Silence stretched between them. Should she say something to him about what she'd been thinking?

Normally, if a girl and a boy wanted to court there was talk back and forth, between their friends at first, then the girl and boy. But she and Roland weren't teens anymore. They didn't really need intermediaries, did they? She looked around. No one was within hearing distance. If she was going to say something, she had to do it now, before she lost her nerve.

"Roland?"

"Ya?"

"I want to talk to you about—"

Johanna took a deep breath and clasped her hands so that Roland wouldn't see how they were shaking. "Roland?" she began.

In his gray eyes, color swirled and deepened. "Yes, Johanna?"

She took another breath and looked right at him. "Will you marry me?"

Books by Emma Miller

Love Inspired

*Courting Ruth
*Miriam's Heart
*Anna's Gift
*Leah's Choice
*Redeeming Grace
*Johanna's Bridegroom

*Hannah's Daughters

EMMA MILLER

lives quietly in her old farmhouse in rural Delaware amid fertile fields and lush woodlands. Fortunate enough to be born into a family of strong faith, she grew up on a dairy farm, surrounded by loving parents, siblings, grandparents, aunts, uncles and cousins. Emma was educated in local schools, and once taught in an Amish schoolhouse much like the one at Seven Poplars. When she's not caring for her large family, reading and writing are her favorite pastimes.

Johanna's Bridegroom
Emma Miller

Recycling programs
for this product may
not exist in your area.

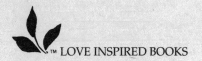 ™ LOVE INSPIRED BOOKS

ISBN-13: 978-0-373-81691-0

JOHANNA'S BRIDEGROOM

www.LoveInspiredBooks.com

Printed in U.S.A.

Love is patient, love is kind. It does not envy,
it does not boast, it is not proud.
—*1 Corinthians* 13:4

Chapter One

Kent County, Delaware
June

Johanna kissed her sister's newborn and inhaled the infant's sweet baby scent before gently placing her into the antique walnut cradle. It was midafternoon, and Johanna, Anna, Rebecca and *Grossmama* were gathered on the screened-in back porch of the Mast farmhouse, enjoying cold lemonade and hulling a bounty of end-of-the-season strawberries to make jam.

Johanna stood over the cradle, gazing down at the baby's long thick lashes, her chubby, pink cheeks and the riot of red-gold curls peeping out from under her antique, white-lace bonnet. Tiny Rose sighed in her sleep, opened one perfect hand, pursed her perfectly formed lips and melted Johanna's heart. Tears blurred her vision. *She's so precious.*

It wasn't that she coveted Anna and Samuel's gift from God. She didn't. But it seemed so long since her own children had been newborns. Jonah, at five, was now old enough to be a real help in the garden and barnyard. And, as he reminded her at least three times a day, he'd be starting school in the fall. Even her chatterbox, Katy, now three, had outgrown her baby smocks and become independent overnight. She was always eager to sweep the kitchen floor with her miniature broom, gather eggs and pick strawberries in the wake of the bigger children.

I want another baby, Johanna admitted to herself. *My arms ache for another child, but having one means marrying again.* And after her unhappy marriage to Wilmer Detweiler, and the tragedy of his suicide, she wasn't certain she had the strength to face that yet.

She knew that the children she had, especially Jonah, needed a father. She and Jonah had always been close, but there were so many things that only a man could teach him—how to plow and trim a horse's hooves, when to cut hay, how to mend a broken windmill. And while Wilmer had been kind to Katy, he'd shown only stern disapproval and constant criticism of Jonah. For all his energy and warm heart, Jonah desperately needed a loving father's guidance. Without it, Johanna feared that Jonah would never fully understand how to grow into a man. And she wasn't the only one who had come to that conclusion. It had been two years since Wilmer's death, and members of the community and her family had been hinting that it was time she remarry. Johanna prayed every night that she would know when the time was right and that God would bring a good man into her life.

"She's adorable, Anna." *Beautiful,* she thought, but she didn't say the word out loud. Physical beauty wasn't something the Old Order Amish were supposed to dwell on. Better a child or an adult have grace and a pure spirit within than a pleasing face.

"And such an easy baby," *Grossmama* said. "Like my Jonas. A *gut* baby." She capped a large crimson strawberry and popped it in her mouth. Closing her eyes, she chewed contentedly, savoring the sweet flavor.

Anna looked up from the earthenware bowl in her lap and smiled with barely contained pride. "Rose is a good baby, isn't she? Poor Samuel can't believe it. He keeps getting out of bed at night to make certain she's still breathing."

Grossmama's eyes snapped open, and she nodded so hard her bonnet strings bounced. "Happy *mudder,* happy *kinner.* And such a quick delivery. Pray that Martha has such an easy birth when her time comes."

"It's Ruth who's expecting," Rebecca gently

reminded her grandmother. "Not Aunt Martha. Our sister Ruth."

Johanna tried not to smile at the thought of Aunt Martha, older than her mother, having a new baby. *Grossmama's* physical health had been good, and she seemed happier since coming to live with Anna, but her memory continued to fail. Not only was she convinced that Anna's husband, Samuel, was her dead son, Jonas, but she mixed up names and people so often that one had to constantly think twice when one had a conversation with her. Only yesterday, *Grossmama* had been certain that Bishop Atlee was her new beau, come to take her to a frolic. Johanna couldn't help wondering what the English at the senior center, where *Grossmama* taught rug making several days a week, thought of their grandmother.

"Are these the last of them?" Rebecca asked. Two brimming dishpans of ripe strawberries stood on the table, waiting to be washed and crushed before being added to the bubbling kettles on the stove.

"No," Johanna said. "I think there's one more flat. I'll go—" She broke off as the pounding of a horse's hooves on the dirt lane caught her attention. "It's Irwin!" She snatched open the screen door and hurried down the wooden steps, wondering why he was in such a hurry.

Blackie galloped into the yard with Irwin, hatless and white-faced, clinging to his bare back. Chickens squawked and flew in all directions as the teenager yanked the gelding up so hard that the horse began to buck, and Irwin nearly tumbled off.

"What's wrong?" Johanna cried. Irwin, the teen who Johanna's mother had adopted, never moved faster than molasses in January. "Ruth's not—"

"Not Ruth! It's Roland's J.J."

Roland. For an instant, Johanna felt paralyzed. *If Roland was in danger, she— No,* she told herself, *not Roland. J.J., Roland's little boy.* The moment passed and she regained her self-control. "What is it?" she demanded.

Irwin half slid, half jumped to the ground, letting the reins slip through his hands. Blackie made one more leap and blew flecks of foam from his mouth and nose. Neck and tail arched, the spirited horse trotted onto the lawn, where, after a few more antics, he began to snatch up mouthfuls of grass.

"You've got to come! *Schnell!*" Irwin steadied himself and ran toward Johanna. "Bees! A swarm! In Roland's tree. They're crawling all over J.J.! Roland says they could sting him to death!"

"Bees?" Johanna asked. "Roland doesn't keep bees." *If J.J. was in danger, she had to go, but how could she go? After everything that lay between them, knowing how she felt, how could Roland ask it of her?* "Are you certain they're honeybees?"

Irwin nodded. "H…honeybees!"

Johanna grabbed him by his thin shoulders and shook him. "Calm down!" she ordered. "Has J.J. been stung?"

"Ne." Irwin shook his head. "Roland doesn't know what to do. He says you have to come. You know bees."

"All right," Johanna agreed. J.J.'s little face, the image of his father, flashed through her thoughts, and she swallowed, trying to keep her voice from showing what she really felt. "You run to our farm," she instructed Irwin calmly. "Get my smoker and my bee suit and an empty nuc box and bring them to Roland's."

He knitted his eyebrows. "What kind of box?"

"A used hive body. A deep one. And don't forget my lemongrass oil. It's on the shelf beside my gloves. Bring them to Roland's." She took a deep breath and pressed her hands to her sides to keep anyone from seeing them tremble. "Can you remember all that?"

He nodded.

"Good. Now run, as quickly as you can!"

Anna and Rebecca had followed her into the yard. "What's happened?" Rebecca asked.

"Irwin says that there's a swarm of bees at Roland's."

"In the tree! By the pond. And…and J.J.'s up in the tree with them," Irwin said. For all his fourteen years, he looked as though he was about to burst into tears. Red patches stood out on his blotchy complexion, and his hay-thatch hair stuck up in tufts. Somewhere, he'd lost his hat, and one suspender sagged.

"Go now," Johanna told Irwin. "And don't stop for anything!"

Irwin took off.

"I've got to go see what I can do," Johanna said to Rebecca and Anna, taking care not to show how flustered she really was. She'd been an apiarist long enough to know that it was important to remain calm with bees. They seemed to be able to sense a person's mood and the best way to calm a hive—or a swarm—was to stay calm herself. *As if that's possible,* the warning voice in her head whispered, *when you have to go to Roland's house and pretend you're only friends.*

"Take one of our buggies," Anna offered. "We'll help you hitch—"

"Ne." Johanna glanced from her sisters to where the horse grazed on the lawn. "There's no time. I'll ride Blackie."

"Bareback?" Anna's eyes widened. "Are you sure? Blackie's—"

"Headstrong. Skittish. I know." Johanna grimaced. "It isn't as if we didn't get thrown off worse when we were kids." *How could she tell Anna that she was afraid? Not of Blackie or of*

*being thrown, but of Roland...of the past she'd
thought she'd put behind her years ago?*

"You're going to ride astride, like a man?" Rebecca shook her head. "It's against the *Ordnung*. Not fitting for women. Bishop Atlee will—"

"J.J.'s life might be in danger. The bishop will understand that this is an emergency," Johanna answered with more confidence than she felt. Her heart raced as she bent and ripped up a handful of grass and walked slowly toward Blackie. The animal rolled his eyes and backed up a few steps, ears pricked and muscles tensed.

"Easy," Johanna soothed. "Good boy. Just a little closer." She inched forward and grabbed a trailing rein. "Give me a boost up," she said to her sisters.

Rebecca shook her head. "You're going to be in *sooo* much trouble."

Ignoring Rebecca, Anna moved to Blackie's side and cupped her hands. Johanna thrust a bare foot into the makeshift stirrup and swung up onto the horse's back.

"Was is?" Grossmama shouted. *"Baremlich!"*

But Johanna had already pulled Blackie's head around, grabbed a handful of mane and dug her heels into the animal's sides. Blackie broke into a trot, and they galloped away.

Roland Byler's stomach did a flip-flop as he stood by the pond and stared up at his only child.

J.J. had climbed into the branches of a Granny Smith apple tree and sat with his back against the trunk and his legs swinging down on either side of a branch. He was at least eight feet off the ground, but the distance ordinarily wouldn't have worried Roland too much. Although J.J. was only four, he was strong and agile, and climbed like a squirrel. He'd been scrambling up ladders and into trees almost since he'd learned to walk. What terrified Roland today was that his son was surrounded by thousands of honeybees.

"Please, God, protect him," Roland murmured under his breath. And louder, to J.J., he called, "Sit still, don't move. Don't do anything to startle them."

J.J. giggled. "Don't be scared, *Dat*. They won't hurt me. They like me." Bees surrounded him, walking on his bare feet, his arms and fingers. They buzzed around his head and face and crawled in his hair. And only inches from J.J.'s head, a wriggling cluster of the winged insects, thicker than the boy's body, swayed on a slender branch.

"Don't make any noise," Roland warned as J.J. began to hum the tune to an old hymn. Roland's heart thudded against his ribs, his skin was clammy-cold and his chest felt so tight that it was hard to breathe. "Do as I say!" he ordered.

When Roland was ten, he'd had a cousin in the Kishacoquillas Valley who'd attempted to rob a honey tree and had been stung to death. Roland shuddered, trying to shut out the memory of the dead boy's swollen and disfigured face as he lay in his coffin.

He couldn't dwell on his poor cousin or his grieving family. The bishop who'd delivered the sermon at his funeral had assured them that the boy was safe with God. Roland knew that was what the Bible taught. This world wasn't important. It was only a preparation for the next, but Roland's faith wasn't always as strong as he would like. His cousin's parents had had six living children remaining when they lost their son. J.J. was all he had. Roland had survived the death of his wife, Pauline, and the unborn babies she'd been carrying, but if he lost this precious son, his own life would be over.

"They tickle." J.J. giggled again. "Climb up, *Dat,* and see how nice they are."

"Hush. I told you not to move." All sorts of wild ideas surfaced in Roland's head. Maybe he could cut down the tree and J.J. could jump free. Or he could tell J.J. to jump into his arms. He'd leap into the pond—washing the bees off them both before they could sting them. But Roland knew that was foolishness. Neither of them could move fast enough. The bees were already crawling all over J.J.

Besides, if Roland startled the swarm, they

might all attack both of them. He didn't care about himself, but his son was so small. The child could be stung hundreds of times in just a minute. Roland's only hope was prayer and the belief that Irwin would return soon with Johanna. She was a beekeeper. She worked with bees every day. If anyone could tell him what to do to save his child, it would be Johanna.

"Dat!" J.J. waved a bee-covered hand and pointed toward the meadow that bordered the road.

Roland looked up to see the Yoders' black horse coming fast across the pasture. But there was no gate along that fence line. Irwin would have to backtrack around by the farmyard to get to the pond. But the boy was galloping straight on toward—

Roland's stomach pitched. That wasn't Irwin on Blackie! The rider wore a blue dress and a white *Kapp. A girl? It couldn't be.* "Johanna?" Roland backed away from the tree and ran toward the fence waving his arms. *Was she blind? Couldn't she see there was no opening? Why hadn't she reined in the horse? Surely, she couldn't mean to...* "No!" he bellowed. "Don't try to jump that—"

But as the words came out of his mouth, Roland saw that it was too late. Blackie soared over the three-rail fence and came thundering down, Johanna clinging stubbornly to his back. She yanked back on the reins, but the horse had the bit between his teeth and didn't slacken his pace. When the gelding didn't respond, she pulled hard on one rein, forcing him to circle left. He dug in his front legs, then tried to rear, but she fought him to a trot and finally to a walk. Johanna pulled up ten feet from Roland and slid down off the horse's sweat-streaked back.

Johanna landed barefoot in the grass and straightened her *Kapp* as she hurried toward him. "Is J.J. all right?" she asked.

Speechless, Roland stared gape-mouthed at her. She was breathing hard but otherwise seemed no worse for her wild careen across the field. All he could think was that she had come. Johanna had come, and she'd find a way to save his son. But what he said was, "Are you crazy? You? A grown woman with two children? To ride that horse bareback like some madcap boy?"

Johanna…the woman who might have been his…who might have been J.J.'s mother if not for one stupid night of foolishness.

"Are you finished?" she asked, scolding him as if he was the one who'd just done something outrageous. Her chin went up and tiny lines of disapproval creased the corners of her beautiful eyes—eyes so piercingly blue and direct that for an instant, he didn't see a delicate woman standing there. In a flash, he saw, instead, Johanna's father, Jonas Yoder, as strong a man in faith and courage as Roland had ever known.

Johanna walked to the base of the tree, her gaze taking in J.J. and the writhing mass of bees above him. "Hi," she called.

"Hi." J.J. grinned at her, despite the two bees crawling over his chin. "Look at all the bees," he said. "Aren't they neat?"

"Very neat," she answered softly. She tilted her head back. "That's a lot of bees."

"A hundred, at least," J.J. agreed.

Roland stifled a groan. "There must be thousands of them," he whispered.

Johanna smiled, ignoring Roland. "You're a brave boy. Some people are afraid of honeybees."

J.J. nodded. "They're nice."

"I think so, too." Johanna glanced back at Roland. A bee lit on her *Kapp,* but she didn't seem to notice. "Do you have a stepladder?"

"In the shed."

"Could you go get it? Irwin should be coming anytime with my bee equipment. When he gets here, bring it to me. Keep Irwin away." She grimaced. "He makes the bees nervous."

"They make *me* nervous." Roland looked from her to J.J. and back at her again. "Are you going to smoke them? I've heard that calms them."

"It probably wouldn't hurt." She glanced back at the swarm. "They've left someone's bee box somewhere, or a hollow tree," she said to J.J. "Or maybe an abandoned building."

"Why did they do that?" the boy asked.

"Probably because their queen was old or the hive got too crowded. They're being so friendly because they don't have honey to protect." She shrugged. "They're just looking for a new home."

"Oh."

"Were they in the tree when you climbed up there?" she asked.

J.J. nodded. "I wanted to see what they were doing."

"He's been singing to them," Roland said, swallowing to try to dissolve his fear. "He just didn't understand how dangerous it was."

"The bees didn't sting me," J.J. said. "They like me."

"Do they like it when you sing?" Johanna asked. And when J.J. nodded, she added, "Then you can sing to them, if you want to. I sing to mine all the time."

J.J. giggled. "You do?"

"The ladder," she reminded Roland as she continued to watch J.J. in the tree.

Roland backed away slowly. He was still sweating and his hands and feet felt wooden, but some of the awful despair that had paralyzed him earlier had ebbed away. *Johanna didn't seem alarmed. Obviously, she had a plan.*

He turned and ran. "Don't leave him."

"Don't worry," she called after him. "We're fine, aren't we, J.J.?"

"Ya, Dat," he heard his son say. "We're fine."

Pray to God you are. Roland lengthened his stride, running with every ounce of strength in his body.

Chapter Two

"Honeybees are wonderful creatures," Johanna told J.J. He nodded, still seemingly unafraid of the dozens of insects crawling in his hair and over his body. J.J. was calm and happy, which was good. Far too many people feared bees, and she had always believed that they sensed when you were afraid. "Do you like honey on your biscuits?" she asked, trying to distract him while they waited for Roland to return with the ladder.

"My *grossmama* makes biscuits sometimes. And my aunt Mary. *Dat* doesn't know how." A mischievous grin spread across J.J.'s freckled face, and he blew a bee off his nose. "*Dat's* biscuits are yucky. He always burns them."

"Biscuits can be tricky if you don't watch them carefully," Johanna agreed. She glanced from the boy to where Blackie grazed. When Roland got back, she'd ask him to catch the horse and walk him until he cooled down. A horse that drank too much cold water when he was hot sometimes foundered.

Absentmindedly, Johanna rubbed her shoulder. It had been years since she'd ridden a horse, and tomorrow she'd feel every day of her twenty-seven years. Not that she'd admit it to Roland or anyone else, but jumping a three-rail fence bareback hadn't been her idea. It had been Blackie's. And by the time she realized that there was no opening in the fence and no gate, it was too late to keep the gelding from going over.

In spite of his high-spirited willfulness, Johanna was fond of Blackie. He had a sweet disposition and he never tried to bite or kick. Despite *Mam's* salary from teaching school, money from the farm, and the income from Johanna's bees, turkeys and quilts, money was always tight. If anything happened to the young driving horse, the family would find it difficult to replace him.

"Here comes *Dat*," J.J. announced.

"Remember to think good thoughts," Johanna said aloud. In her head, she repeated the thought over and over.

"J.J., did you know that a community of bees thinks all together, like they have one brain?" she asked him, in an attempt to keep her composure, as well as help him keep his. "This swarm has drones and workers and, in the middle, a queen.

The others all protect her, because without the queen, there can be no colony."

"Why did they land in this tree in a big ball?"

"They're looking for a new home. For some reason, and we don't know why, they couldn't live in their old house anymore. They won't stay here in the tree. They need to find a safe place where they can store their honey, protect the queen and safely raise baby bees."

"Uncle Charley said that when a honeybee stings you, it dies."

Johanna nodded. "Uncle Charley's right. But a bee won't sting unless it's afraid, afraid you'll hurt it or that you'll harm the hive. That's why we stay calm and think happy thoughts when we're near the bees."

"They like me to sing to them."

She smiled at J.J., wondering how so much wisdom lived in that small head. "Who taught you about bees?"

The little boy's forehead wrinkled in concentration, and Johanna's heart skipped a beat. She'd seen that exact expression a hundred times on Roland's face. *You think you can put the past behind you, but you can't.* All this time, she'd been telling herself that she didn't care anymore. And she'd been wrong. Her throat clenched. She'd loved Roland Byler for more than half her life, and in spite of everything he'd done to destroy that love, she was afraid that some part of her still cared.

"Nobody told me," J.J. said solemnly. "Bees are my friends."

Johanna nodded. "You know what I think, J.J.? I think God gave you a special gift. I think you're a bee charmer."

"I am?" He flashed another grin. "A bee charmer. That's me."

Roland halted behind Johanna with the ladder over his shoulder. "Where do you want this? I brought some old rags and matches, in case you want to try to smoke the swarm."

"No sign of Irwin?" Johanna looked back toward the house. "He should have been here by now."

"I saw your buggy coming up the road. He'll be here in a few minutes." Roland glanced up at his son. "Are you all right? No stings?"

"Ne, Dat." J.J. grinned. "I told you. Bees never sting me."

Roland frowned. "I don't know what possessed you to climb up in that tree when you saw them. You should have better sense."

"Atch, Roland," Johanna said, as she put a proper mental distance between them. "He's a child. He's naturally curious. You don't see bees swarm every day."

"It would suit me if I never saw another one. I don't like bees. I never have."

"Then it's best if you stand back from the tree," she cautioned. "If you're afraid, they'll sense it. It might upset them."

"I can't see that bees have much sense about anything," Roland said. "How big can their brains be?"

"They're smart, *Dat*. Johanna said they pro… pro what the queen."

"Protect," Johanna supplied.

"Protect the queen," J.J. repeated with a grin.

"No need to fill the boy's head with *lecherich* nonsense." Roland used the Pennsylvania Dutch word for ridiculous. "Just get him down out of there safely."

Johanna rolled her eyes and reached for the ladder. "Let me do that. You might startle them."

"Don't you want to wait for your equipment?"

"I'm not going to need it," she said, eyeing the swarm. "J.J. and I are doing just fine. Give me the ladder."

Roland opened the wooden stepladder and set it on the ground. "It's too heavy for you to lift," he muttered.

Johanna bit back a quick retort. *Men! She might not be as tall and sturdy as her sister Anna, but she was strong for her size. Who did he think lifted the bales of hay and fifty-pound bags of sheep-*

and turkey food? And who did he suppose moved her wooden beehives?

She lifted the ladder onto her shoulder and carried it slowly over to the apple tree. "Sing to the bees, J.J.," she said. "What do they like best?"

In a high, sweet voice, the child began an old German hymn. Johanna settled the legs of the ladder into the soft grass and put her foot on the bottom rung. She joined in J.J.'s song.

"Let me steady that for you," Roland offered.

She shook her head. "*Ne.* Let them get used to me." She began to sing again as she slowly, one step at a time, climbed the ladder. When she was almost at the top, she put out her arms. "Swing your leg over the branch," she murmured. "Slowly. Keep singing." J.J. did just as she instructed, and she nodded encouragement. "Easy. That's right."

As J.J. put his arms around her neck, she blew two bees off his left cheek.

He broke off in the middle of the hymn and giggled. "They tickle."

Instantly, the sound of the swarm's buzzing grew louder.

Behind her, Johanna could hear Roland's sharp intake of breath. "Come to me," she murmured. "Slowly. Keep singing." Another bee took flight, leaving the child's arm to join the main swarm. She caught J.J. by the waist, and the two of them waited, unmoving, as bees crawled out of his hair and flew into the branches above them. She brushed two more bees off his right arm. "Good. Now we'll start down. Slow and steady."

Sweat beaded on the back of Johanna's dress collar and trickled down her back. Step by step, the two of them inched down the ladder, and it seemed to Johanna that the tone and volume of the colony's buzzing grew softer.

As J.J.'s bare feet touched the earth, the last bee abandoned the child's mop of yellow-blond hair and buzzed away. "Go on," Johanna said to the boy. "It's safe now. Go to your *dat*."

She threw Roland an *I told you so* look, but her knees felt weak. She hadn't thought the boy was in real danger, but one could never be certain. And she knew that had anything bad happened to J.J., she would have felt responsible. She'd been frightened for the boy, nothing more, she told herself. And all those silly thoughts about Roland and what they'd once meant to each other could be forgotten. They could go on as they had, neighbors, members of the same church family, friends—nothing more.

A shout from the direction of the barnyard and the rattle of buggy wheels bumping over the field announced Irwin's arrival. "If you don't mind, Roland, I'll set up a catch-trap on the bench there. The water is what drew the swarm here in the first place. And if I can lure them into the nuc box, I can move the whole colony back to our place."

When he didn't answer, she glanced at him. No wonder he hadn't heard her. Roland's full attention was on his child. He was still hugging J.J. so hard that the boy could hardly catch his breath.

"Unless you'd like to keep the bees," Johanna added. "I've got an extra eight-frame hive that I'm not using. I could bring it over and teach you how to—"

"You take the heathen beasts and are welcome to them," Roland replied.

"If you're sure, I'll be glad to have them. But it'll take a few weeks for the colony to settle in to a new hive, before I can move them. Of course I have to lure them into it first."

"Whatever you want, Johanna." His dashed the back of his hand across his eyes. "Thank you. What you did was…was brave. For a woman. For anyone, I mean. You saved J.J. and I won't forget it."

Johanna ruffled the boy's hair. "I think he would have been just fine," she said. "The bees like him."

J.J. grinned.

"But you'll keep well away from them in the future," Roland admonished.

"Obey your father," Johanna said.

"But I don't want to stay away from them," the child said. "I want to see the queen."

Roland gave him a stern look. "You go near them again and—"

"Mam! Mam!"

Johanna looked back to see Jonah, wearing his bee hat and protective veil netting, leaping out of their buggy. "I remembered the lemongrass oil, *Mam,*" he shouted. "Irwin forgot, but I remembered."

J.J. wiggled out of his father's grasp and stared in awe at Jonah's white helmet. Jonah saw the younger boy and positively strutted toward the tree.

It was all Johanna could do not to laugh at the two of them. She raised a palm in warning. "Thank you for the lemongrass oil, Jonah, but you won't need the hat. These bees have had enough excitement for one day." She gave her son *the look,* and his posturing came to a quick end.

"Hi, J.J.," Jonah said as he removed the helmet and tucked it under his arm. "Did you get stung? Where's the swarm?"

J.J. pointed, and the two children were drawn together as if they were magnets. Immediately, J.J., younger by nearly two years, switched from English to Pennsylvania Dutch and excitedly began relating his adventure with the bees to Jonah in hushed whispers.

"Both of you stay away from the swarm," Johanna warned as she directed Irwin and Roland to carry the wooden hive to the bench beside the water. Irwin lifted off the top and she used the scented oil liberally on the floor of the box. "Hopefully, this will draw the bees," she explained to Roland as they all backed away. "Now we wait to see if they'll decide to move in. We'll know in a day or two."

"I brought your suit and the smoker stuff," Irwin said.

"*Danke,* but I don't think I'll need it," Johanna answered. "I didn't know what I'd find." She looked around and saw that Jonah and J.J. had caught the loose horse. "You can take Blackie for me, Irwin. Jonah and I can drive the buggy home."

She watched as the teenager used the buggy wheel to climb up on the horse's back and slowly rode toward the barnyard.

"Can I drive the buggy home, *Mam?*" Jonah asked.

Johanna laughed. "Down the busy road? I don't think so." Jonah's face fell. "But you can drive back to Roland's house, if you like." Nodding, Jonah scrambled back up into the buggy, followed closely by J.J.

"Don't worry," Johanna said to Roland. "They're perfectly safe with our mare Molly." It was easier now that the crisis had passed, easier to act as if she was just a neighbor who'd come to help... easier to be alone with Roland and act as if they had never been more than friends.

"*Dat,* I'm hungry," J.J. called from the buggy seat.

Jonah nodded. "Me, too."

"I guess you are," Roland said to J.J. as he and Johanna walked beside the buggy that was rolling slowly toward the barnyard. "We missed dinner, didn't we? I think we have bologna and cheese in the refrigerator. You boys go up to the house. Tie the mare to the hitching rail and you can make yourselves a sandwich."

J.J. made a face. "We're out of bread, *Dat*. Remember? The old bread got hard and you threw it to the chickens last night."

Roland's face flushed. "I'll find you something."

"How about some biscuits?" Johanna asked, walking beside Roland. "If you have flour, I could make you some."

"*Ya!* Biscuits!" J.J. cried.

Roland tugged at the brim of his hat. "I wouldn't want to put you out. You've already—"

"Don't be silly, Roland. What are neighbors for? I can't imagine how you and J.J. manage the house and the farm, plus your farrier work, just the two of you."

"Mary helps with the cleaning sometimes. I'll admit that I don't keep the house the way Pauline did."

"It won't be the first messy kitchen I've ever seen. Let me bake the biscuits," Johanna said, eager now to treat Roland as she would any neighbor in need of assistance. "And whatever else I can find to make a meal. If it makes you feel any better, Jonah and I will share it with you. It's the least I can do for your gift of a hive of bees."

"A gift you're more than welcome to." He offered her a shy smile, and the sight of it made a shiver pass down her spine. Roland Byler had always had a smile that would melt ice in a January snowstorm.

"The thought of homemade biscuits is tempting," he said. "There's a chicken, too, but it's not cooked."

She forced herself to return his smile. "You and the boys do your chores and give me a little time to tend to the meal," she said briskly.

"Don't say I didn't warn you about the kitchen. I left dirty dishes from breakfast and—"

"Hush, Roland Byler. I think I can manage." Chuckling, she left him at the barn and walked toward the house.

An hour later, the smell of frying chicken, hot biscuits, green beans cooked with bacon and new potatoes drew Roland to the house like a crow to newly sprouting corn plants. The boys followed close on his heels as he stopped to wash his hands and splash cold pump water over his face at the sink on the back porch. Straw hat in hand, Roland stepped into the kitchen and was so shocked by its transformation that he nearly backed out the door.

This couldn't be the same kitchen he and J.J. had left only a few hours ago! Light streamed in through the windows, spilling across a still-damp and newly scrubbed floor. The round oak pedestal table that had belonged to his father's grandmother was no longer piled high with mail, paperwork, newspapers and breakfast dishes. Instead, the wood had been shined and set for dinner. In the center stood a blue pitcher filled with flowers and by each plate a spotless white cloth napkin. Where had Johanna found the napkins? In the year since Pauline's death, he hadn't seen them. But it wasn't flowers and pretty chinaware that drew him to the table.

"Biscuits!" J.J. said. "Look, Jonah! Biscuits!"

"Let me see your hands, boys," Johanna ordered.

Jonah and J.J. extended their palms obediently, and Roland had to check himself from doing the same. Self-consciously, he pulled out a ladder-back chair and took his place at the table. Both boys hurried to their chairs.

On the table was a platter of fried chicken, another of biscuits, an ivory-colored bowl of green beans and another of peaches.

"I thought it best just to put everything on the table and let us help ourselves," Johanna said. "It's the way we do it at home. I found the peaches and the green beans in the cellar. I hope you don't mind that I opened them."

"Fine with me." Roland's mouth was watering and his stomach growling. Breakfast had been cold cereal and hard-boiled eggs. Last night's supper had consisted of bologna and cheese without bread, tomato soup out of a can and slightly stale cookies to go with their milk. He hadn't sat down to a meal like this since he'd been invited to dinner at Charley and Miriam's house the previous week. Roland was just reaching for a biscuit when Johanna's husky voice broke through his thoughts.

"Bow your heads for the blessing, boys. We don't eat before grace."

"Ne," Roland chimed in, quick to change his reaching for a biscuit motion to folding his hands in silent prayer. *Lord, God, thank You for this food, and thank You for the hands that prepared it.* He opened one eye and saw that Johanna's head was still modestly lowered. He couldn't help noticing that the hair along her hairline was peeping out from under her *Kapp* and had curled into tight, damp ringlets. Seeing that and the way Johanna had tied up her bonnet strings at the nape of her neck made his throat tighten with emotion.

Refusing to consider how pretty she looked, he clamped his eyes shut and slowly repeated the Lord's Prayer. And this time, when he opened his eyes again, the others were waiting for him. Johanna had an amused look on her face, not exactly a smile, but definitely a pleased expression.

"Now we can eat," she said.

Roland reached for the platter of chicken and passed it to her. "You didn't need to clean my dirty kitchen, but we appreciate it."

"I did need to, if I was to cook a proper meal," she replied, accepting a chicken thigh. "It's no shame for you to leave housework undone when you have so much to do outside. I'm only sorry you haven't asked for help from the community."

"We manage, J.J. and I."

"Roland Byler. You were the first to help when Silas lost the roof on his hog pen. You must have the grace to accept help as well as give it. You can't be so stubborn."

"You think so?" he asked, stung by her criticism. Personally, he'd always thought that *she* was the stubborn one. True, he had wronged her and he'd embarrassed her with his behavior back when they'd been courting. He'd tried to apologize, more than once, but she'd never really accepted it. One night of bad choices, and she'd gone off and married another.

"Dat?" J.J. giggled. "You broke your biscuit."

Roland looked down to see that he'd unknowingly crushed the biscuit in his hand. "Like it that way," he mumbled as he dropped it onto his plate and stabbed a bite of chicken and a piece of biscuit with his fork.

"Gut chicken," J.J. said.

"If you don't eat all those biscuits, you can have one with peaches on it for dessert," Johanna told the boys. "If you aren't full, that is."

"We won't be, *Mam*," Jonah said. "I never get tired of your biscuits."

And I never get tired of watching you, Roland thought as he helped himself to more chicken. But he was building a barn out of straw, wishing for what he couldn't have, for what he'd thrown away with both hands in the foolishness of his youth.

Johanna's kind acts of cleaning his kitchen and cooking dinner for them had been the charitable act of one neighbor to another, nothing more. And all the wishing in the world wouldn't change that.

Chapter Three

At nine the following Saturday morning, Johanna stood in the combined kitchen-great room of the new farmhouse that her sisters Ruth and Miriam shared. Ruth and Eli had the downstairs. Miriam and Charley occupied an apartment on the second floor, but the two couples usually took their meals together and Ruth cooked. Miriam preferred outdoor work, and Ruth enjoyed the tasks of a homemaker. It was an odd arrangement for the Amish, one that Seven Poplars gossips found endlessly entertaining, but it worked for the four of them.

"Miriam?" Johanna called up the steps. "Are you ready? Charley has the horse hitched."

Today, *Mam,* most of Johanna's sisters and the small children were all off on an excursion to the Mennonite Strawberry Festival, a yearly event that everyone looked forward to. Their sister Grace, who still lived at home but attended the

Mennonite Church, owned a car. She'd graciously offered to drive some of them, and *Mam,* Susanna, Rebecca, Katy and Aunt Jezzy had already gone ahead with her. But there were too many Yoders to fit in Grace's automobile, so Miriam was driving a buggyful, as well. Anna loved the Strawberry Festival, but since Rose was so tiny, Anna had decided to remain at home and keep Ruth company. Ruth was in the last stage of pregnancy with twins and preferred staying close to home and out of the heat.

"I feel bad going off and leaving the two of you," Johanna said. "We had such a good time last year."

Ruth settled into a comfortable chair and rubbed the front of her protruding apron. "Until these two are born, I don't have the energy to walk to the mailbox, let alone chase my nieces and nephews around the festival."

Anna smiled and switched small Rose, hidden modestly under a receiving blanket, to her other breast. The baby settled easily into her new position and began to nurse. "Don't worry about us," Anna said. "You're so sweet to take my girls. They've been talking about it all week."

"No problem. And your Naomi is such a big help with Katy." Johanna threw a longing glance at the baby. "First Leah, then you, and Ruth in a month. It will be Miriam next, I suppose."

"Miriam next for what?" Anna's twin sister came hurrying down the steps in a new rose-colored dress, her prayer cap askew and her apron strings dangling.

"Kapp," Ruth reminded.

Miriam rolled her eyes, straightened her head covering and tied her apron strings with a double knot behind her waist. "Satisfied?"

"Ya." Ruth, always the enforcer of proper behavior when out among the worldly English, nodded. "Much better."

"And what is it I'm next for?" Miriam asked, unwilling to have her question go unanswered.

Anna chuckled again. "A *boppli,* of course. A baby of your own. A little wood chopper for Charley or a kitchen helper."

Miriam shrugged. "In God's time. We haven't been married that long. And it took Ruth and Eli ages to get around to it." She glanced at Johanna with a gleam of mischief in her eyes. "How do you know it will be me? Maybe it will be *your* turn next. Look at you. You've got that look on your face when you hold Rose. You can't wait to be a mother again."

"She's right," Ruth agreed. "You've mourned Wilmer long enough. It's time you married again."

"To whom?"

Miriam laughed. "You know who. I've heard

you've been at his place three times this week.
And cleaned his house."

"Only the kitchen. And he was only there the
first day, the day J.J. was up the tree with the
bees. The other two times he was off shoeing
horses. I had to go check on the new hive. The
swarm moved into my nuc box, and I'm getting
free bees." Johanna knew she was babbling on
when she should have held her tongue. Arguing
with Miriam always made things worse.

"I see," Miriam said. "You're going to *take care
of the bees.*"

"Exactly. It doesn't have anything to do with
Roland." Johanna sighed in exasperation. The
trouble with being close to her sisters was that
they knew everything. Nothing in her life was
private, and all of them had an opinion they were
all too willing to share. And the fact that they'd
touched on a subject that had kept her awake late
for the past few nights made her even more uncomfortable. First, she had to make up her own
mind what she wanted. Then she would share her
decision. "Who told you I went over to Roland's
three times? Rebecca or Irwin?"

Ruth chuckled. "Just a little bird. But we're serious. It's not good for your children to be without
a father. You know Roland would make a good
dat. Even *Mam* says so. Roland owns his farm.
No mortgage. And such a hard worker. He'll be a

good provider. And don't forget he's got a motherless son. You two should just stop turning your backs on each other and get married."

"Before someone else snaps him up," Miriam quipped. "At Spence's, I saw one of those Lancaster girls giving him the once-over. At the Beachys' cheese stall. '*Atch,* Roland,'" she mimicked in a high, singsong voice. "'A man alone shouldn't eat so much cheddar and bologna in one week. Is not *gut* for your health. What you need is a wife to cook for you.'"

Johanna flushed. It was too warm in the house. She went to the door and opened it, letting the breeze calm her unease. In the yard, Grace's son, 'Kota, hung out the back door of Charley's buggy, and Anna's Mae bounced on the front seat. She couldn't see Anna's Lori Ann or Jonah, but she could hear Naomi telling them to settle down. "It's not as easy to know what to do as you think," Johanna said to her sisters. "People change."

"You haven't changed," Anna put in quietly. "What you felt for Roland years ago, that was real. It's not too late for the two of you."

Johanna looked back at Anna. "You think I should fling myself at him?"

Ruth folded her arms over her chest with determination. "It's plain as the nose on your face that he still cares for you. If you weren't so stubborn, you'd see it."

"What happened before…between you and him…it hurt you," Anna continued. "I remember how you cried. But Roland was young then and sowing his oats. Can't you find it in your heart to forgive him?"

Not forgive, but forget. Could I ever trust him again?

"Miriam!" Charley shouted from outside. "Come take this horse! I don't trust these kids with this mare, and I can't stand here all day holding her. I've got work to do."

"Go. Have fun," Ruth said. "But promise me you'll think about what we said, Johanna."

"Please," Anna said. "We only want what's best for you and your children."

"So do I," Johanna admitted. "So do I."

The Mennonite school, where the festival was held, wasn't more than five miles away. *Mam* and Grace and the others were there when Johanna and her crew arrived. Jonah and 'Kota were fairly bursting out of their britches when Miriam turned the buggy into the parking lot, and Anna's girls appeared to be just as excited. A volunteer came to take the children's modest admittance fees and stamp the back of their hands with a red strawberry. That stamp would admit them to all the games, the rides, the petting zoo featuring baby farm animals, a straw-bale mountain and maze and a book fair where each child could choose a free book.

"There's Katy!" Jonah cried, waving to his little sister. Katy and Susanna were riding in a blue cart pulled by a huge, black-and-white Newfoundland dog. Following close behind trudged a smiling David King, his battered paper crown peeking out from under his straw hat. David was holding tight to a string. At the end of it bobbed a red strawberry balloon.

"I want a balloon!" Mae exclaimed. "Can I have a balloon?"

"If you like," Johanna said. "But your *Mam* gave you each two dollars to spend. Make sure that the balloon is what you really want before you buy it."

"I want a balloon, too," 'Kota declared. "A blue one."

"Strawberries aren't blue," Jonah said loftily.

"Uh-huh," 'Kota replied, pointing out a girl holding a blue strawberry balloon on a string.

Johanna smiled as she helped the children out of the buggy and sent them scurrying safely across the field that served as a parking lot. Despite his olive skin and piercing dark eyes, Grace's little boy looked as properly plain as Jonah. The two cousins, inseparable friends, were clad exactly alike in blue home-sewn shirts and trousers with snaps and ties instead of buttons, black suspenders and wide-brimmed straw hats. No one would recognize 'Kota as the thin, shy, undersized child who'd first appeared at *Mam's* back door on that rainy night last fall. *Another of God's gifts.* Life was full of surprises.

"Over here," *Mam* called. "Why don't you leave the girls with us? I imagine Lori Ann, Mae and Naomi would like to ride in the dog cart."

"There's J.J.," Jonah shouted. "Hey, J.J.! He's climbing the hay bales. Can we—"

"I promised Naomi we'd go to the book fair first," Miriam said, joining them. "Grace is working there all morning. Don't worry about the horse. Irwin's going to see that the mare gets water and is tied up in the shed. Do you mind if we go on ahead, inside?"

Quickly, the sisters made a plan to meet at the picnic tables in two hours. Children were divided; money was handed out and Johanna followed 'Kota and Jonah to the entrance to the straw-bale maze. From the top of a straw "mountain," J.J. waved and called to them. The area was fenced, so she didn't have to worry about losing track of her energetic charges. Johanna found a spot on a straw bale beside several other waiting mothers and sat down. Since J.J. was here, Johanna was all too aware that Roland couldn't be far away. She glanced around, but didn't see him.

Her sisters' advice about Roland echoed many of her own thoughts. Years ago, she and Roland...

No, she wouldn't think about that. So many memories—some good, some bad—clouded her judgment. She had prayed over her indecision, but if God had a plan for her, she was too dense to hear His voice. Sometimes her inner voice whispered that she didn't need another husband, that she and the children were doing just fine. But at other times, she was assailed by the wisdom of hundreds of years of Amish women who'd lived before her.

Amish men and women were expected to marry and live together in a home centered on faith and family and community. Remaining single went against the unwritten rules of her church. Even a widow, like her mother, was supposed to remarry. Mourning too long was considered selfish. *Dat* and Wilmer, to put a fine point on it, had both left this earth. It was her duty and her mother's duty to continue on here on earth, following the *Ordnung* and remaining faithful to the community.

Johanna knew, in her heart of hearts, that it was time she found a new husband. She didn't need Anna or Ruth or even her mother to tell her that. Looking at it from the church's point of view, she had to first find a man of faith, a man who would help her to raise her children to be hardworking and devoted members of the community. Second, as a mother, she should pick someone who would set a good example, and hopefully a man who could support her and her children—those she already had and those they might have together. She hadn't needed her sisters to offer that advice, either. She was very good at making logical decisions.

If she married Roland, she honestly believed that she wouldn't have to worry about struggling to feed and clothe her children. His farrier business was thriving. She knew that Roland, unlike Wilmer, would never raise his hand to her in anger. And she was certain that he didn't drink alcohol or use tobacco, both substances she abhorred. Johanna shivered as she remembered the last time Wilmer had struck her. She was not a violent woman, but it had taken every ounce of her willpower not to fight back. Instead, she'd waited until he fell into a drunken sleep, gathered her babies and fled the house.

She pushed those bad memories out of her head. With Roland, she would be safe. Her children would be safe. They wouldn't grow up under her mother's roof without a father's direction. And Roland, unlike Wilmer, would be a man both she and the children could respect.

Two English girls ran out of the maze together. The women beside Johanna stood and walked away with the laughing children. Johanna glanced back at the straw mountain, saw the boys and sank again into her thoughts.

Many Amish marriages were arranged ones. And many couples who came together for logical reasons, such as partnership, sharing a similar faith and pleasing their families, came to care deeply for each other. As far as she could tell, most of the English world married for romantic love and nearly half of those unions ended in divorce.

The Amish did not divorce. Had she been forced to leave Wilmer and return to her mother's home permanently, both of them would have been in danger of being cast out of the church—shunned. Under certain circumstances, she could have remained part of the community, but they would still have been married. As long as the two of them lived, there could be no dissolving the marriage.

Marrying a man for practical reasons would be a sensible plan. If each of them kept their part of the bargain, if they showed respect and worked hard, romantic love might not be necessary. She considered whether she would find Roland attractive if they had just met, if they hadn't played and worked and worshiped together since they were small children. How would she react if he wasn't Roland Byler, Charley and Mary's older brother, if she hadn't wept a butter churn full of tears over him? What would she do if a matchmaker told *Mam* that a widowed farmer named Jakey Coblentz wanted to court Johanna?

The answer was as plain as the *Kapp* on her

head. She would agree to meet this Jakey, to walk out with him, to make an honest effort to discover if they were compatible. So why, when she valued her mother's and her sisters' opinions, had she been so reluctant to consider Roland? To forget what had happened? She closed her eyes and pictured his features in her mind.

"Don't go to sleep," a familiar male voice said.

Johanna's eyes flew open and she jumped so hard that she nearly fell off the bale of straw. Roland stood directly in front of her, holding two red snow cones. "Roland."

He laughed and handed her one of the treats. "It's strawberry. If I remember, you like snow cones. Any flavor but blue." He took a bite of his own.

She searched for something to say. In desperation, she grabbed the snow cone and took a bite. Instantly, the cold went straight to her brain and she felt a sharp pain. "Ow!"

He laughed at her, sat down beside her and reached over and wiped a granule of ice off her chin. "You always did do that," he reminded her.

"Let me pay you for this," she stammered.

"*Ne.* Enjoy. I bought it for J.J."

Johanna gasped. "I'm eating J.J.'s snow cone?"

Roland shrugged. "I'll buy him another one. Now that 'Kota and Jonah are up there…" Roland indicated the top of the straw slide. "With him, it would just go to waste. It would be a puddle of strawberry syrup by the time he got to eat it." He grinned. "So you're doing me a favor. Keeping me from wasting a dollar."

"Oh." She still felt flustered.

"That was smart—what you did with the bees. They went into the box you put out for them."

Bees were a safe subject. Tentatively, she took another nibble of the snow cone. It was delicious. She couldn't remember when she'd had one last. Whoever had made it had ground real strawberries into the juice. She fixed her gaze on the ground. Roland was wearing new leather high-top shoes. Black. His trousers were clean, but wrinkled. *Very* wrinkled. They needed a good pressing.

"I've always been afraid of bees," he said.

She licked at the flavored ice. "I know."

"J.J. seems fascinated by them. He asks me all kinds of questions—questions I can't answer."

She took another bite, chewed slowly and swallowed. "I think he's a bee charmer. They won't hurt him. You don't have to worry."

"I found the biscuits you left for us on the kitchen table Thursday. And the potato soup. They were good, really good."

"I'm glad you liked them." A dribble of strawberry water ran down her hand onto her wrist. She passed the paper cone into her other hand and licked up the stray drop. "Messy," she murmured.

"Good stuff is."

Silence stretched between them. Shivers ran down her arms. Should she say something to him about what she'd been thinking? About the two of them? Normally, if a girl and a boy wanted to court, there was talk back and forth, between their friends at first, then between the girl and boy themselves. But she and Roland weren't teens anymore. They didn't need intermediaries, did they? She looked around. No one was within earshot. If she was going to say something, she had to do it now, before she lost her nerve.

"Roland?"

"Ya?"

"I want to talk to you about—"

"Johanna! Johanna! Did you see? King David and me! We rode in the blue cart." Johanna's sister Susanna appeared in front of them, laughing merrily. "No horse. A dog. A dog pulled the cart! Did you see us ride?"

David, glued to Susanna's side, smiled and pointed at Johanna's snow cone. "Ice cream? I like ice cream."

David, like Susanna, had Down's syndrome but was harder to understand. Johanna could usually follow what he was saying. He was a good-hearted boy, always smiling, and Johanna liked him.

"Ne," Susanna said. "Not a ice cream cone. A

snow cone." She stared longingly at Johanna's. "Can we have one?"

"I don't like snow. To eat it," David said.

"You'll like it," Susanna assured him.

"I'll buy you snow cones." Roland reached into his pocket.

"You have money, Susanna," Johanna reminded her. "*Mam* gave you five dollars. Did you spend it all?"

Susanna shook her head.

"It's nice of Roland to offer, but you need to buy your own. And buy David one, too."

Rebecca joined them, with Katy in tow. Katy looked longingly at Johanna's snow cone.

"Here," Johanna said. "Have the rest of mine, Katy. Or get Susanna to buy you one. She and David were just headed to the snow cone booth."

Rebecca glanced from Johanna to Roland and back. Johanna could almost see the wheels turning in her sister's head.

"Ah," Rebecca said. "I think we need to find snow cones for Susanna and David. Can you help me, Katy?"

Johanna's fingertips tingled and her chest felt tight. Maybe this wasn't the time. Maybe Susanna and David's interruption had kept her from doing something she'd regret. "I'll come with you," she said.

Rebecca chuckled. "No need. You two *old* people

sit here in the sun. I think I saw the snow cone stand by the school."

Roland pointed. "It's by the gym doors, but if you don't have enough—"

Susanna waved her five-dollar bill. "I have money," she said. "Come on, King David." She started off and, again, David followed.

Rebecca looked back at Johanna. "Have fun, you two," she teased. "Come on, Katy. Would you like to see the baby lambs?"

Roland watched the four of them walk away. "Smart, your sisters," he said. "All of them."

Johanna smiled at him. "*Ya.* All of them," she agreed. "Susanna, too."

He nodded. "I always thought so. A credit to your parents, that girl."

Johanna took a deep breath and clasped her hands so that Roland wouldn't see how they were shaking. "Roland?" she began.

In his gray eyes, color swirled and deepened. "Yes, Johanna?"

She took another breath and looked right at him. "Will you marry me?"

Chapter Four

Once, when he was eighteen and learning his trade as a farrier, Roland had been kicked by a stallion his uncle was shoeing. The blow had been so quick and hard that Roland was picking himself up off the ground almost before he'd realized that he'd been struck by a flying hoof. He hadn't lost consciousness, but for what seemed like an eternity, he hadn't been able to think straight.

Johanna's matter-of-fact question had much the same effect. He was stunned. "What did you say?" he stammered. Around him, the laughter and happy shrieks of the children, the red balloon that had come loose from its mooring and was floating skyward, and the sweet smell of ripe strawberries faded. For a long second, Roland's whole world narrowed to the woman sitting beside him.

Johanna rolled her eyes. "Are you listening to me? I asked if you would marry me."

He swallowed, opened his mouth to speak and then took a big gulp of air. "Did you just ask me to marry you?" he managed.

She folded her hands gracefully over her starched black apron. "It's the logical thing for us to do," she answered.

He heard what she said, but his attention was fixed on the red-gold curls that had come loose from her severe bun and framed her heart-shaped face, a face so fresh and youthful that it might have belonged to a teenage girl instead of a widow and mother in her late twenties. Johanna's skin was fair and pink, dusted with a faint trail of golden freckles over the bridge of her nose and across her cheeks. Her eyes were the exact shade of bluebells, and her mouth was... Roland swallowed again. He'd always thought that Johanna Yoder had the prettiest mouth—even when she'd been admonishing him for something he'd done wrong.

They had a long history, he and Johanna...a history that he'd hoped and prayed would become a future. In the deepest part of his heart, he'd wanted to ask her the very question that she'd just asked him. But now that she'd spoken it first, he was poleaxed.

"Do I take that as a *no?*" she asked, as a flush started at her slender throat and spread up over her face. "You don't want to marry me?"

He could hear the hurt in her voice, and his

stomach clenched. Johanna's voice wasn't high, like most young women's. It was low, husky and rich. She had a beautiful singing voice. And when she raised that voice in hymns during Sunday worship service, the sound was so sweet it almost brought tears to his eyes.

Abruptly, she stood.

"*Ne,* Johanna. Don't!" He caught her hand. "Sit. Please."

Clearly flustered, she jerked her hand away, but not before he felt the warmth of her flesh and an invisible rush of energy that leaped between them. The shock of that touch jolted him in the same way that his skin prickled when a bolt of lightning struck nearby in a thunderstorm. He'd never understood that, and he still didn't, but he felt it now.

"You know I want to marry you," he said, all in a rush, before he lost his nerve. "I've been waiting for the right time…when I thought you were—"

"Through mourning Wilmer?" Johanna's blue eyes clouded with deep violet. She lowered her voice and glanced around to see if anyone was staring at them.

Roland found himself doing the same. But the children were busy climbing the mountain of straw, and no one else seemed to have noticed that the ground under his feet was no longer solid and his brain had turned to mush. He returned his gaze to her. "To show decent respect for my Pauline and your—"

"Deceased husband?" She made a tiny shrug and her lips firmed into a thin line. "Wilmer was my husband and the father of my children. We took marriage vows together, and if…" She took a deep breath. "If he hadn't passed, I would have remained his wife." She shook her head. "I'd be speaking an untruth if I told you that there was love or respect left in my heart for him when he died—if there wasn't the smallest part of relief when I knew he'd gone into the Lord's care. I know it's a sin to feel that way, but I—"

"Johanna, you don't have to—" he began, but she cut him off with a raised palm.

"*Ne,* Roland. Let me finish, please. I'll say this, and then we'll speak of it no more. Wilmer was not a well man. His mind was troubled. But the fault in our marriage was not his alone. I've spent hours on my knees asking for God's forgiveness. I should have tried harder to help him…to find help for him."

One of Johanna's small hands rested on the straw bale between them, and he covered it with his own and squeezed it, out of sympathy for her pain. This time, she didn't pull away. He waited, and she went on.

"You know I was no longer living under Wilmer's roof when he died. His sickness and his drinking of spirits made it impossible for me to remain there with my children." Johanna raised her eyes to meet his gaze, and Roland saw the tears that her pride would not allow to fall.

A tightness gathered in Roland's chest. "Did he... Was Wilmer..." A rising anger against the dead man threatened to make him say things he might later regret. As Johanna had said...as Bishop Atlee had said, Wilmer's illness had robbed him of reason. He was not responsible for what he did, and it was not for any of them to judge him. But Roland had to ask. "Did he ever hit you?"

Johanna turned her face away.

It was all the answer he needed. Roland wasn't a violent man, but he did have a temper that needed careful tending. If Wilmer had appeared in front of them now, alive and well, Roland wasn't certain he could have refrained from giving him a sound thumping.

Johanna's voice was a thin whisper. "It was Jonah's safety that worried me most. When Wilmer..." A shudder passed through her tensed frame. "When he began to take out his anger on our son, I couldn't take it any longer. I know that it's the right of a father to discipline his children, but this was more than discipline." She looked back, meeting Roland's level gaze. "Wilmer got it into his head that Jonah wasn't his son, but yours."

"Mine?" Roland's mouth gaped. "But we never… you never…"

Johanna sighed. "Exactly. I've been accused of being outspoken, too stubborn for a woman and willful—all true, to my shame. But, you, above all men, should know that I—"

"Would never break your marriage vows," he said. "Could never do anything to compromise your honor or that of your husband." He fought to control the anger churning in his gut. "In all the time we courted, we never did anything more than hold hands and—"

"We kissed once," she reminded him. "At the bishop's husking bee. When you found the red ear of corn?"

"We were what? Fifteen?"

"I was fifteen," Johanna said. Her expression softened, and some of the regret faded from her clear blue eyes. "You were sixteen."

"And as I remember, you nearly knocked me on my—"

"I didn't strike you." The corners of her mouth curled into a smile. "I just gave you a gentle nudge, to make you stop kissing me."

"You shoved me so hard that I fell backward and landed in a pile of corncobs. Charley told on me, and I was the butt of everyone's jokes for months." He squeezed her hand again. "It wasn't much of a kiss for all that fuss, but I still remember how sweet your lips tasted."

"Don't be fresh, Roland Byler," she admonished, once again becoming the no-nonsense Johanna he knew and loved. "Remember you are a grown man, a father and a baptized member of the church. Talk of foolishness between teenagers isn't seemly."

"I suppose not," he said grudgingly. "But I never forgot that kiss."

She pulled her hand free and tucked it behind her back. "Enough of that. We have a decision to make, you and I. I've thought about it and prayed about it. I've listened to my sisters chatter on the subject until I'm sick of it. You are a widower with a young son, and I'm a widow with two small, fatherless children, and it's time we both remarried. We belong to the same church, we have the same values, and you have a farm and a good job. That we should marry and join our families is the logical solution."

Logical? He waited for her to speak of love…or at least to say how she'd always cared for him… to say that she'd never gotten over their teenage romance.

"What?" she demanded. "Haven't I put it plainly? We both have to marry someone. And you live close by. We're already almost family, with your brother Charley and my sister Miriam already husband and wife. You have plenty of room for my sheep and bees. I think that empty shed would be perfect for my turkey poults."

"Turkeys? Bees?" He stood, backed away, and planted his feet solidly. "I'd hoped there'd be a better reason for us to exchange vows. What of affection, Johanna? Aren't a husband and wife supposed to—"

Her eyes narrowed, and a thin crease marred her smooth forehead. "If you're looking for me to speak of romance, I'm afraid you'll be disappointed. We're past that, Roland. We're too old, and we've seen too much of life. Don't you remember what the visiting preacher said at Barbara and Tobias's wedding? Marriage is to establish a family and strengthen the bonds of community and church."

Pain knifed through him. All this time, he'd been certain that Johanna felt the same way about him that he felt about her. Not that he'd ever betrayed his late wife—not in deed and not in thought. He'd kept Johanna in a quiet corner of his heart. But now he'd thought that they'd have a second chance. "It was my fault, what happened between us. What went wrong…I've never denied it. I know how badly I hurt you, and I'm sorry. I've been sorry ever since—"

"Roland. What are you talking about? We were kids when we walked out together. Neither of us had joined the church. That's the past. I'm not clinging to it, and you can't, either. It's time to look to our future. What we have to do is decide if we would be good for each other. We're both hard workers and we're both dedicated to our children. It seems silly for me to look elsewhere for a husband when you live so close to my mother's farm."

"So we're to decide on the rest of our lives because my land lies near your mother's?" He hesitated, realizing his words were going to get him into trouble. But he couldn't help how he felt and he wouldn't be able to sleep tonight if he didn't express those feelings. "I take it that you'd want to have the banns read at the next worship service. Since you've already made up your mind, why wait? Widows and widowers may marry when they choose. Why waste time with courting when you could be cleaning my house and your sheep could be grazing in my meadow?"

"Are you being sarcastic?"

"Answer me one question, Johanna. Do you love me?"

She averted her eyes. "I'm too old and too sensible for that. I respect you, and I think you respect me. Isn't that enough?"

"No." He shook his head. "No, it isn't." Where had this gone so wrong? He had pictured the two of them riding out together in his two-seater behind his new trotter, imagined them taking the children to the beach, going to the State Fair together this summer. He badly wanted to court Johanna properly, and she'd shattered all his hopes and dreams by her emotionless proposal. "It's not enough for me. And it shouldn't be enough for you."

She pursed her lips. "Well, that's clear enough. I'm sorry to have troubled you, Roland. It's plain that we can't—"

"Can't what? Can't find what we had and lost? Pauline was a sensible match that suited both our families. In time, when J.J. came, love came and filled our house. When I lost her, part of my heart went with her. But I won't marry for convenience, not again. If the feelings you have for me aren't deep and strong, you'd be better to find some other candidate, some prosperous farmer or tradesmen who would be satisfied with a sensible wife. Because…because I'm looking for more."

Red spots flared on Johanna's cheeks. "It's good we had this talk. Otherwise, who knows how much time we would have wasted when we should be looking for—"

"I hope you find what you're searching for," Roland said. "And when you find a man willing to settle for a partnership, I hope you're happy."

She folded her arms over her chest. "You don't find happiness in others. You find it in yourself and in service to family and community."

"So you're saying I'm selfish?"

"I didn't mean it that way."

"It sounds as if that's exactly what you meant." With a nod, he turned to search for his son and walked away. There was nothing more to say, nothing more he wanted to hear. He wanted to make Johanna his wife. He could think of no one who would be a more loving mother to J.J., but not under these circumstances…never under these circumstances.

"I'm glad we got this straightened out," she called after him. "Because it's clear to me that the two of us would never work out."

Johanna's temper was out of the box now. She was mad, but he didn't care. Better to have her angry at him than to feel nothing at all.

Later that evening, at the forge beside his barn, Roland shaped a horseshoe on his anvil, with powerful swings of his hammer. Sparks flew, and his brother Charley chuckled.

"Just make it fit, Roland," Charley teased. "Don't beat it to death."

It was after supper, but Roland hadn't taken time to eat. He'd been hard at work since he'd left the festival. Not wanting to spoil J.J.'s day, he'd given permission for Grace to keep him with her boy, 'Kota, and bring him home in the morning. Since tomorrow wasn't a church Sunday, it would be a leisurely day for visiting. Hannah Yoder, Johanna's *mam,* had invited him to join them for supper tonight, but after the heated words he and Johanna had exchanged, her table was the last place he wanted to be.

Besides, Roland was in no mood to be a patient father this evening.

Charley had apologized for bringing his mare to be shod so late in the day. "I wouldn't have bothered you, but I promised Miriam we'd drive over to attend services in her friend Polly's district. You know Polly and Evan, don't you? They moved here from Virginia last summer."

Roland did know Evan Beachy. The newcomer had brought a roan gelding to be shod just after Christmas. Evan was a tall, quiet man with a gentle hand for his horses. Roland liked him, but he didn't want to make small talk about the Beachys from Virginia. He wanted to get Charley's opinion on what had gone wrong between Johanna and him.

Charley was always quick with a joke, but he and his brother were close. Under his breezy manner, Charley hid a smart, sensible mind and a caring heart. Roland had to talk to somebody, and Charley and he had shared their successes and disappointments since they were old enough to confide in each other.

"Brought you some lamb stew," Charley said.

"And some biscuits. Figured you wouldn't bother to make your own supper. You never did have the sense to eat regular."

"If I ate as much as you, I'd be the size of LeRoy Zook."

Charley pulled a face. "Don't try to deny it. You don't eat right. What did you have for breakfast?"

"An egg-and-bologna sandwich with cheese."

"And dinner? Did you even have dinner today?"

Roland didn't answer. He'd had the strawberry snow cone. He'd had every intention of asking Johanna if she'd join him for the chicken-and-dumpling special that the Mennonite ladies were offering, but after their disagreement, he'd lost his appetite.

"So, no dinner and no supper. You're a pitiful case, brother. Good thing that I remembered to bring you Ruth's lamb stew. She made enough for half the church."

"I appreciate the stew and biscuits, but I can do without your sass," Roland answered.

When the shoe was shaped to suit him, Roland pressed it to the mare's front left hoof to make certain of the fit, then heated it and hammered it into place. Last, he checked the hoof for any ragged edges and pronounced the work sound. He released the animal's leg, patted her neck, and glanced back at his brother.

"I've ruined it all between Johanna and me,"

he said. And then, quickly, before he regretted his confession, he told Charley what had happened earlier in the day. "She asked me to marry her," he said when he was done with his sad tale. "And fool that I am, I refused her." He raised his gaze to meet his brother's. "I don't want a partner," he said. "I couldn't go into a marriage with a woman who didn't love me—not a second time. Pauline was a good woman. We never exchanged a harsh word in all the years we were married, but I was hoping for more."

Charley removed the sprig of new clover he'd been nibbling on. "You love Johanna, and you want her to love you back."

Roland nodded. "I do." He swallowed, but the lump in his throat wouldn't dissolve. He turned away, went to the old well, slid aside the heavy wooden cover and cranked up a bucket of cold water. Taking a deep breath, he dumped the bucket over his head and sweat-soaked undershirt. The icy water sluiced over him, but it didn't wash away the hurt or the pain of the threat of losing Johanna a second time. "Was I wrong to turn her down, Charley? Am I cutting off my nose to spite my face? Maybe I would be happier having her as a wife who respects me, but doesn't love me, instead of not having her at all."

Charley tugged at his close-cropped beard, a beard that Preacher Reuben disapproved of and even Samuel had rolled his eyes at, a beard that some might think was too short for a married man. "You want my honest opinion? Or do you just want to whine and have someone listen?"

"You think I've made a terrible mistake, don't you? Say it, if that's what you think. I can take it."

Charley came to the well, cranked up a second bucket of water and used an enamel dipper to take a drink. Then he poured the rest of the bucket into a pail for the mare. She dipped her velvety nose in the water and slurped noisily.

Roland wanted to shake his brother. In typical fashion, Charley was taking his good old time in applying the heat, letting Roland suffer as he waited to hear the words. Finally, when he'd nearly lost the last of his patience, Charley nodded and glanced back from the mare.

"You're working yourself into a lather for nothing, brother. Don't you remember what a chase Miriam gave me? 'We're friends, Charley,'" he mimicked. "'You're just like a brother.' Do you think I wanted to be Miriam's friend? I loved her since she was in leading strings, since we slept in the same cradle as nurslings. Miriam was the sun and moon for me. It's not right for a Christian man to say such things, but sinner that I am, it's how I feel about her. But you know what men say about the Yoder girls."

Roland nodded. "They're a handful."

"It's true," Charley agreed. "From Hannah right down to Rebecca. Even Susanna, one of God's sweetest children, has her stubborn streak."

"But they're true as rain." Roland ran his fingers through his wet hair. "Strong and good as any woman I've ever met, and that includes our sister Mary."

"Exactly. Worth the trouble, and worth the wait." He smiled. "You know I've never been a betting man. The preachers say the Good Book warns against wagering, and I take that as gospel. But if I was an Englishman without a care for his soul, I'd risk my new Lancaster buggy against a pair of cart wheels that you and Johanna will be married by Christmas next. Mark my words, brother. Everyone in the family knows it. The two of you will come to your senses and work this out. And if you don't, I'll grow my beard out as long and full as Bishop Atlee's himself."

Chapter Five

At nine-thirty on Tuesday morning, Johanna tied Blackie to a hitching rail under a shady tree at the back of one of the buildings at Spence's Auction and Bazaar. Some people didn't bother to remove the bridles of their animals at market, but *Dat* had taught her differently. If a horse had to stand for hours, he didn't need a bit in his mouth. The halter was just as secure and more comfortable for the horse. Any animal deserved respect and loving care, especially one who served so faithfully in pulling the carriage and helping with farm work.

After Johanna had watered Blackie and double-checked his tie rope, she took her split-oak market basket, containing a dozen jars of clover honey, and carried it through the milling shoppers to the family booth.

This spring, the Yoders had had been blessed to take over the space of another Amish family, who was moving to Iowa. The stand was inside a three-sided shed, a little smaller than what they'd had outside, but in an excellent location and sheltered from the weather. Sometimes they sold vegetables from *Mam's* garden, and—depending on the season—they offered honey, homemade jams and preserves, pickles and relishes, and holiday wreaths. And since they'd acquired the new, shaded booth, Aunt Jezzy had taken over running the table with help from whichever Yoder sister was available.

Going to Spence's two days a week and selling to strangers was a big step for Aunt Jezzy because she was naturally shy around the English. *Mam* had secretly wondered if it wasn't too much to expect of her, but after a few weeks, Aunt Jezzy had really taken to the job and had proved to be an excellent businesswoman. Her cashbox always balanced out to the penny, and she quickly became popular with customers and other sellers.

Grace had dropped Aunt Jezzy and Rebecca off early that morning on her way to the local community college, where she was studying to be a veterinary technician, but her classes didn't let out until five today. Johanna would have to remain until afternoon to drive her aunt and sister home when they closed the booth. Usually, Johanna brought Katy or Jonah or both with her, but since they'd gone to spend the day at Anna's, she was alone.

The weather was warm and sunny, and there seemed to be a lot of people at Spence's that morning. As Johanna entered the open building with her heavy basket, she was pleased to see several regular customers standing at the table, and her display of honey and beeswax lip salve and soap nearly gone. Aunt Jezzy was counting out change to an older man, and Rebecca was bagging the last pint of strawberries, berries that Susanna had picked before breakfast.

How pleased her little sister would be to add to the savings she kept in a hen-shaped crockery jar under her bed. This morning, Susanna had whispered that she was going to buy *Mam* a birthday present. Of course, last week, she'd wanted Charley to buy her a pink pig with black spots, and at supper last night, she'd announced that she wanted a big dog and a cart, so she and King David could drive it to Dover every day. Susanna always had plans, but no matter how they turned out, she was always happy.

Susanna is truly blessed with a loving spirit, Johanna thought. *She was born with the grace I've always struggled to find.*

Rebecca glanced up and smiled. "Hi. We were wondering where you were. Your bee-tending took longer at Roland's than you expected?" she said in Pennsylvania *Deutch*.

Johanna ignored her sister's teasing remark. "It

was a busy morning," she said, once the customers had been waited on and moved on. "You've sold a lot."

"Ya," Aunt Jezzy agreed as she spun the closed moneybox exactly three complete rotations before stashing it safely under the table. "Most of Susanna's strawberries went right away," she said, continuing on in the same dialect. Aunt Jezzy's English was excellent, but she always preferred Pennsylvania Dutch when they were alone or with other Amish. "Without Rebecca's help, I would have been hard-pressed. She is a good girl, your sister. Always kind to me and your *grossmama,* Lovina, when she and Leah stayed with us in Ohio."

"I think we did so well because a tourist bus from Washington stopped," Rebecca explained, switching the conversation back to English. "Some of the people started staring and asked silly questions, but then Leah's husband's aunt Joyce came over. She spoke up, saying how the salve was organic. One lady bought a lip balm and tried it right away. And then the others started buying."

"They snapped up those fancy half-pint jars of honey, too," Aunt Jezzy said. "And never argued about the price." She chuckled. "But they talked loud, like I was deaf."

"You handled them perfectly," Rebecca said. "You should have seen her, Johanna. *Schmaert.*

Smiling, and so quaint." Rebecca giggled. "*Vit* a heavy *Deutch* accent. And when one Englisher whipped out her cell phone to take a photograph of her, Aunt Jezzy turned her back. She refused to wait on anyone else. Then the bus driver blew his horn to leave, and the other tourists made the woman put her cell away so they could buy before they had to go."

Aunt Jezzy's cheeks glowed rosy with pleasure at the praise. "Maybe it's not this *narrisch* old woman. Maybe your sister Rebecca is why you sold so many of those salves and soaps. She made those pretty labels with her good handwriting. And it's good that she can talk so easily to the English."

Rebecca beamed. "It's wonderful honey," she said. "It sells itself. Johanna does all the work."

"I think the bees do most of it," Aunt Jezzy said.

"God's handiwork." Rebecca smiled. "You're right to remind us, Aunt Jezzy. We receive so many blessings from Him every day."

Johanna nodded and busied herself arranging the jars of honey she'd brought with her. She could always trust Rebecca to remember what was important. The two of them hadn't been as close as they might have been when they were growing up. Rebecca had been younger and unwilling to listen to a bossy older sister, and Johanna feared she'd underestimated Rebecca.

But since Leah had married Daniel and gone away to South America to be a Mennonite missionary, Rebecca had stepped in to fill the empty place in Johanna's heart. Why had she never realized how wise Rebecca was? Strong in her faith and always willing to turn a hand to what needed doing, Rebecca reminded Johanna so much of their mother.

But Rebecca would marry soon and start her own family, Johanna thought. She might move away, as well. Johanna didn't want to dwell on that. She'd never liked change, and she needed her family around her, all of them, even Aunt Jezzy, *Grossmama* and their new sister, Grace, and 'Kota. *If only I could keep them all close to me.*

Rebecca brushed Johanna's hand with her own. "The past few years have been difficult for you, I know," she murmured. "But the Lord never deserted you, even in your darkest hour."

Johanna nodded, too full of emotion to speak. Her sister's words were true. Her own life might be in turmoil, but she had never felt deserted by His mercy. He had kept her and her children safe from Wilmer's rage, and He had provided a refuge for them in the arms of her family.

Johanna couldn't imagine what she would have done if her mother hadn't welcomed her and her children into her home. Sometimes, Johanna thought that the easiest thing to do would be to remain there under her mother's roof, supporting Jonah and Katy by selling her quilts, her wool, her turkeys and her honey.

Aunt Jezzy had never married, and she never seemed to mind. She went her own way, tapping on wood, spinning her coffee cup three times before she added her sugar, talking to herself when she was alone and always wearing violet-colored dresses. In spite of her nonconformity, she seemed unconcerned by what others thought of her and was always smiling. Maybe some of the Yoder women were meant to follow a different path.

"Rebecca didn't have time to get her breakfast," Aunt Jezzy said, tugging Johanna from her thoughts. "You two go along and have a good chat. It's slower now. I'll be fine until you get back."

"Are you sure?" Rebecca asked, but she tucked her pencil and small notepad into her apron pocket.

For years, Rebecca had been a faithful correspondent, submitting Kent County happenings to the *Budget,* the paper subscribed to and read by Amish and Mennonites all over the world. Her sister had never signed her name, simply putting *Your Delaware Neighbor* at the bottom of her submissions. The *Budget* shared news of new neighbors, farms sold, visitors, births, illnesses, weddings and deaths. It was a way for those apart from the world to remain connected to each other and, in her small way, Rebecca helped to hold the larger Amish community together.

"We won't be long," Johanna promised her aunt. "I came to help, not to sit and visit and drink iced tea."

"Take your time," Aunt Jezzy urged with a wave. "You work too hard, both of you. You're young. Enjoy yourself for once."

As soon as they were out of their aunt's earshot, Rebecca asked, "So, was he there this morning when you went to tend your bees?"

"Ne." Johanna shook her head. "His sister Mary was there with J.J. Did you know that she's walking out with Donald Troyer? They rode home from the Kings' last Sunday night."

"I hadn't heard." Rebecca's eyes sparkled with mischief. "But you know Mary. She never stays long with one boy. She told me she doesn't want to marry for years yet. She's having too much fun."

Johanna waited, knowing Rebecca would ask.

"So, Roland hasn't spoken to you since he turned you down on Saturday?"

"I'd rather not talk about Roland Byler."

Rebecca made a face. "You want to talk about him. You know you do."

Johanna shook her head again. She did, she supposed, but Rebecca shouldn't be able to see through her so easily. "It was mortifying. I never would have asked him to marry me, if I thought he'd refuse. I was so sure that he…that he cared for me."

"It must have been awful for you." Rebecca stopped to look at a pewter sugar bowl and pitcher for sale. "Pretty, aren't they?"

"You could buy them for your hope chest." Johanna checked the bottom. There was no price marked. "How much for the set?" she asked the woman behind the table. The shape was graceful but simple, perfect. An Amish kitchen was plain, but there were no rules on dishes or tableware. It was a set that Johanna would have loved on her own counter.

When the clerk quoted a price, Rebecca nodded. "I'll think about it."

"It might be gone when you come back," the seller, a pleasant Asian-American woman in a red straw hat and sunglasses, said.

"I know," Rebecca answered. "But I need to decide if I want them." She walked on and Johanna followed.

"If you like the creamer and sugar bowl, you should make an offer," Johanna urged. "Nice things don't last long, not when the sale is so busy."

Rebecca arched an eyebrow. "Could it be the same with good men? If you wait too long to decide, does someone else snap them up?"

"Roland. You're talking about Roland." Johanna's mouth firmed. "I asked him to marry me. What else can I do?"

Rebecca stopped and looked at her. "Maybe you didn't ask him the right way." She gestured to an open doorway, and Johanna followed her outside, into an alley that ran between two buildings. Rebecca glanced both ways, and—when she saw that they were alone—said, "Everyone thinks you're the sensible Yoder girl, the one with the good head on your shoulders. Practical Johanna. They don't know you the way your family does. You're smart, but sometimes you come off too strong, too unemotional. It makes people think you don't feel things. In here." She touched the place over her heart. "Maybe Roland wants a courtship. Maybe he's not so practical. Maybe he wants romance."

"Romance? At our age?"

"Don't be so quick to knock romance," Rebecca said. "Even men can be sentimental."

Johanna frowned. "Could it be that *my* asking *him* upset him? That he thinks I'm too forward for a woman?"

"I doubt that. He's known you all your life. He knows you speak your mind." Rebecca considered. "Did you ever think that Roland might be as scared as you of remarrying? He lost his wife, and he's been hurt, maybe more than you have, because she never hurt him like…"

"Like Wilmer," Johanna supplied. "It's all right. We can be honest with each other."

"*Ya,* we know what Wilmer was like before he passed. Some of it, but you didn't share everything that happened."

"I couldn't. I was ashamed."

"I understand," Rebecca agreed. "But Roland isn't Wilmer. Roland is sweet like Charley. You know how Charley feels about Miriam. Can you blame Roland for wanting to be sure? For wanting the kind of love match his brother has?"

Johanna swallowed. For a moment, all her fears rose inside her.

Rebecca gripped her arm. "And what about you? Are you certain you're ready to remarry? Can you turn your life over to another man? To accept him as head of your family? To obey him?"

"It's the right thing to do...the sensible thing for our children."

"And you always have to be *sensible,* don't you?" Rebecca asked.

"I don't know." Johanna clenched her damp hands. "I suppose it's in my nature. And Ruth and Miriam and Anna are sure Roland and I would make a good marriage. Even *Mam* thinks—"

"*Mam* isn't marrying him. It has to be you," Rebecca said. "Maybe when you're sure...with your heart—not just your head—maybe then, Roland would say yes."

"And if he doesn't?"

Rebecca's eyes brimmed with compassion. "Then you wait until God sends you another opportunity."

"How long?"

Rebecca shrugged. "I don't know. Maybe until the cows come home or you're as old as Aunt Jezzy." She motioned toward the lunchroom. "Now let's eat. I'm starving."

Johanna nodded again. Another moment, and she'd have been in tears. And she didn't want to go back to Aunt Jezzy with red eyes, because their aunt would want to know what was wrong.

Together they went into the noisy food building. It was filled with mingling strangers and at least a dozen Amish. They were lucky enough to find a couple leaving a table and sat down. Rebecca opted for a soda and a roast-beef-and-cheese sandwich.

"That's breakfast?" Johanna teased. She was sticking to iced tea, heavy on the sugar.

Rebecca laughed. "This is what the English call brunch. I ordered cheese fries for Aunt Jezzy. You know how she loves them."

"Guder mariye!" Lydia Beachy waved and came toward them, three children in tow. "How is your mother?"

Johanna found a chair for her mother's friend and they each took a little one on their laps while the adults shared news of the past week. After a few moments, Johanna suggested that they'd better get back to help Aunt Jezzy with the stand.

"I just saw her," Lydia said. One of her older children joined them, and Lydia doled out money for pizza and lemonade. "She was talking to Nip Hilty. You know Nip, don't you? He has the harness shop on Peach Basket Road." Lydia rolled her eyes. "Saw them talking last Friday, too."

"Nip Hilty?" Rebecca asked. "Didn't his wife die last fall?"

"*Ne.*" Lydia leaned closer to Johanna. "Two years ago, Bethany passed. A good woman. Came to our quiltings sometimes. Her heart, I think, but Bethany carried some weight on her. Like me." Lydia patted her rounded abdomen.

Lydia herself was tall and thin with a wide, smiling mouth and a prominent nose. Lydia was definitely not and probably never would be a fat woman, Johanna thought. And if Lydia was gaining weight in the middle, it probably meant that she was expecting another baby. But there wasn't a woman in Kent County with a better heart, unless it was Anna or *Mam.* Lydia was so sweet that people naturally told her everything about everyone. Lydia sifted through the gossip and only passed on what was good and what she believed was true. And if Lydia was hinting at something between Aunt Jezzy and this Nip Hilty, it must have been commonly talked about in the Amish community and generally approved of.

"I've always thought the world of your aunt," Lydia said. "Since your *grossmama* went to live with Anna and Samuel, Jezebel has really perked up. Wouldn't it be something if she found herself a beau at her age?"

Rebecca exchanged glances with Johanna. "Maybe we should get back to work."

"You go on," Lydia urged. "You take a look and see if I'm not right. Like as not, Nip will still be there. Last week, he stood there the better part of an hour, talking her ear off. And Jezzy didn't seem to mind, not one bit."

"What do you think?" Rebecca asked when they were far enough from the lunch area that Lydia could no longer hear them. "She'd never... Not Aunt Jezzy. I just can't imagine..."

Johanna kept walking. She'd make no judgment until she saw them together with her own eyes. It didn't seem possible. Aunt Jezzy was even shyer around Amish men than she was around the English, in general. Johanna had rarely heard her speak to Anna's husband, Samuel, and he certainly wasn't a stranger in the Yoder house. The only male she regularly spoke to was Irwin.

"I don't know what started that talk," Rebecca continued, "but I don't think that she would... would..."

Johanna stopped so quickly that Rebecca nearly bumped into her. There, behind the table, was

Aunt Jezzy, and leaning against a post, eating an ice cream cone, was Nip Hilty. Aunty Jezzy's cheeks were pink and her eyes were sparkling. She was talking up a storm, and Nip Hilty was laughing. And in Aunt Jezzy's hand was a half-eaten double-dip strawberry ice cream cone—a treat she certainly hadn't bought herself.

Chapter Six

"Have you heard anything about Aunt Jezzy and Nip Hilty?" Johanna asked her mother. The two of them were in the kitchen, just finishing preparing supper. Since she, Rebecca and Aunt Jezzy had been at Spence's during the midday meal, *Mam* had gone to more trouble than usual tonight. She'd roasted three fat hens and had made fresh peas and dumplings to go with loaves of dark rye bread, German potato salad, garden salad and a counter full of peach pies. Susanna had already set the table, with Katy's help, and the two of them had gone out to call Irwin, Jonah and 'Kota in to wash up.

"I've met Nip," *Mam* answered, "but I think you and Rebecca must be hatching chickens out of turnips. I can't imagine that Aunt Jezzy would like him in any way other than someone to exchange neighborly talk with."

Johanna glanced toward the door to see Rebecca, her arms full of wildflowers, push open the screen door and enter the kitchen. Once they'd returned home from the sale, Rebecca had changed out of her good dress and had exchanged her *Kapp* for a blue kerchief. Her eyes were shining, her bare feet were dusty and bits of leaves were caught in her hair.

"The flowers are beautiful," Johanna said, admiring the bouquet of yellow oxeye daisies, evening primrose and marsh marigold mixed with the vivid blues of wild lupine and Jacob's ladder. "But you look like you lost a tussle with a banty hen."

Rebecca laughed. "They don't call them wildflowers for nothing. Some are pretty tough."

Mam joined in the easy laughter. "Here, you can put them in this tin pitcher. They'll look nice on the supper table."

Rebecca dumped the flowers and greenery in the sink and began to cut the stems to fit the flowers in the tin pitcher. Of all of them, Rebecca had the greatest gift for growing and arranging flowers. She'd gathered the blooms in less than half an hour.

"I haven't seen the lupine yet this year," Johanna said. "The blue looks so pretty against the yellow of the daisies. Where did you find them?"

"The usual places—the edge of the orchard, behind the barn," Rebecca replied. "But don't change the subject. I heard you say something about me, and I want to know what."

"Nothing bad," *Mam* assured her.

Johanna chuckled. "I was telling *Mam* about Aunt Jezzy and Nip Hilty—about how we were sure he bought her that ice cream cone."

Rebecca glanced at their mother. "If you'd been there, *Mam,* you would think the same thing. She was so relaxed with him, not shy the way she usually is, but all giggly and rosy-cheeked. I'm telling you, Aunt Jezzy has a beau."

Mam folded her arms and shook her head. "You two. You're worse than Martha for gossip. If Jezzy hasn't found a match to suit her in all these years, I doubt she'll change her mind now."

"I'm just saying, it looked suspicious." Rebecca added water to the pitcher and set the arrangement in the center of the white tablecloth. "In a good way," she added. "It would be wonderful if Aunt Jezzy did find a husband, don't you think? She's never had her own home. She's such a good person. She deserves to be happy."

Mam looked from one of them to the other and pursed her lips. "Better the two of you concern yourselves with finding your own husbands." Johanna knew her mother was teasing them, but there was always a thread of truth in *Mam's* jests.

"Not me," Rebecca protested. "I'm too young to get married."

The sound of a car engine caught Johanna's attention. She went to the window to see Grace drive cautiously across the barnyard and park her automobile in the shed. "I can't get used to that motor vehicle coming and going," Johanna remarked. "But I suppose Grace needs it to get to school."

"It will only be here a few more months," *Mam* said, "until her wedding. And I'm sure you'll miss her when she's gone."

"We all will," Rebecca agreed. "We all love her, but it's awkward sometimes, explaining to other Amish why we have a car in our shed and an Englisher living in our house."

"She isn't an Englisher," *Mam* corrected gently. "Grace is a Yoder, and she and her son have as much right to be in your father's house as any of us."

Rebecca's expression grew instantly contrite. "I was lacking in charity to say that, wasn't I?"

"It's no more than what I've thought a hundred times." Johanna sliced the still-warm loaves of bread with a serrated knife. "But *Mam* is right. Grace is our sister, and she belongs here. I didn't mean to be unkind. It's just…"

"Just that change comes hard…for all of us," *Mam* agreed. "I agree that our life was simpler before Grace came, but maybe simple isn't God's plan for us. Maybe loving one another when it isn't easy makes us grow."

Mam removed her work apron and replaced it with a freshly ironed one as white as her starched *Kapp.* She went to the door and opened it wide. "Come in, child," she called. "You're late tonight, but just in time for the evening meal."

From across the yard, Johanna heard the laughter of her daughter and the noisy chatter of Grace's 'Kota and her Jonah. Irwin was a few yards behind them, strolling along in his awkward long-legged gait, but keeping pace with a smiling Susanna.

How could I think of leaving this happy house? Of risking my children's happiness to marry Roland, or any man for that matter? Her years with Wilmer had been tumultuous, and despite her efforts and her tears, she'd never been able to provide the warmth and security her mother's home provided for them all. Jonah and Katy had both blossomed here in this big house. The once-quiet Katy never stopped chattering, and Jonah had changed from a sad child to a bundle of energy.

I should be more like Mam. I have a good enough example. It wasn't enough that Mam was widowed with seven daughters to raise. She not only managed with us and the farm, but she'd opened her arms to Irwin and Grace and 'Kota. She opened her arms to me….

Katy came running into the kitchen. "I found a duck egg!" she cried. "Look, *Grossmama!* And I carried it myself!" She thrust the egg out. "Aunt Susanna says I can have it for breakfast tomorrow!"

"Better you let me beat your egg into pancakes," Rebecca suggested. "Duck eggs are rich and make nice batter."

The two boys spilled into the room on Katy's heels, and Johanna sent them along to wash their hands. She greeted Grace, heard Irwin's tale of an escaped pig and agreed with Susanna that more people were coming every day to borrow books from the tiny lending library that she managed in the old milk house. And in the familiar bustle and routine of the supper hour, Johanna was able to forget her worries about the future and lose herself in the here and now.

Soon the family gathered around the table and lowered their heads for silent prayer. Even Katy and the two boys understood the need to give thanks to God for all the blessings He had bestowed on them. A sense of peace flowed though Johanna. The cares of the world seemed far away.

Once grace was over, everyone began to help themselves to the delicious food. "Wonderful bread," Aunt Jezzy proclaimed. "And your dumplings are light enough to float up to the ceiling."

"Why would they do that?" Susanna asked, poking at a dumpling with her fork. "I want them to stay on my plate so that I can eat them." Everyone smiled at that, and Susanna laughed.

I am truly blessed, Johanna thought. *To be born into this family and faith.* She promised herself that she would try harder to be worthy of them.

"So," *Mam* said to Aunt Jezzy, "the girls say you have an admirer. Nip Hilty. Isn't he a bachelor?"

Aunt Jezzy flushed a bright pink and giggled like a teenager.

"Maybe he's the reason you're so eager to tend the table on sale days," *Mam* suggested.

Aunt Jezzy peeked up through her lashes and spun her water glass exactly three rotations. "He bought me ice cream," she said. "Strawberry." She smiled. "And that's all I'll say about Nip tonight."

The following morning, Johanna and Katy followed the winding path that led across the field from *Mam's* house to Ruth and Eli's. It was a beautiful morning. The sun was shining and last night's shower made the world smell new and fresh in a way that brought tears to Johanna's eyes. *I couldn't imagine not living close to the earth. How do people in cities breathe, let alone thrive?*

Bees buzzed around the honeysuckle in the hedgerow, and the clover was soft under their bare feet. Johanna paused and knelt down to catch Katy in her arms and hug her tightly. "I love you," she murmured. "I love you so much."

"I love you, too, *Mam,*" the child echoed in her sweet voice. "I love you more than the moon."

Off to her left she saw Charley digging post holes for his new fence line. "Morning, sister," he called to her. Johanna waved back. Secretly, she was glad that Charley was busy and wasn't at the house. Charley was as close as a brother to her, and it certainly wasn't his fault that Roland had proven to be so difficult, but making small talk with him this morning would have been awkward.

Since Ruth had gotten so large with the coming twins, Johanna and Rebecca tried to come over at least one day a week to help her with the housework. Miriam and her husband, Charley, lived upstairs, but Miriam—always happier outside than in—spent her days working the farm beside her husband.

As they entered the house, Johanna could smell Ruth's coffee. Katy ran to her and gave her a hug. "Wait until you see what I have," Ruth said. She opened the pantry door, and there in a laundry basket, Johanna saw her sister's orange tabby with three tiny kittens.

"Ooh," Katy said. "Can I hold one?"

Ruth squatted awkwardly and picked up a fuzzy black kitten with white paws and a white spot on its chest. "You can touch it. Gently," she instructed. "But they are too young for you to hold yet. Next week you can hold them." Ruth glanced back. Johanna nodded. "And, if you do just as I tell you, if you are very, very responsible, you can have one of the kittens as soon as it's old enough to leave the mother."

"I can? For my own?" Katy wiggled with joy. "*Mam?* Can I?"

"You heard your aunt Ruth. You must show her that you know how to take care of a *bussli*. A kitten is a big responsibility. You must feed it and take it outside and keep it safe until it's large enough to take care of itself."

"She's a sensible child," Ruth said after they'd left Katy to admire the kittens and gone out to sit on Ruth's screened-in porch with their coffee. "You've done a wonderful job with her. You're a fine mother. I only hope I can do as well."

"You?" Johanna chuckled. "You'll be a far better mother than me."

Ruth rubbed the front of her apron. "I can't wait. It doesn't seem possible. Eli and I...after we lost..." She sighed. "I worry that everything will be all right, Johanna. I don't know how I'd bear it if something went wrong."

"We must trust in God. You're healthy. The babies have strong heartbeats." Johanna had gone to the midwife with Ruth on her last checkup and heard the heartbeats herself. "There's no reason to be afraid. Enjoy your last days of peace and quiet. With twins, you and Eli won't get a full night's sleep for at least two years."

Ruth laughed. "If I ever complain, remind me

that I prayed for this." For a few moments, they sat in silence, listening to a Carolina wren scolding a jay that approached too close to the wren's nest under the porch eaves. They watched the sunshine sparkle on the dewdrops that lingered on the hollyhocks, savoring the quiet companionship of sisters who were best friends.

And then Ruth broke the comfortable solitude by saying, "Dorcas came by yesterday afternoon. She told me that Roland asked you to marry him and you turned him down flat."

Johanna nearly choked on her mouthful of coffee. "What?" she sputtered. "Who told her that?" Their cousin Dorcas could be a bit of a gossip.

The expression in Ruth's nutmeg-brown eyes grew serious. "Is it true? Did you turn him down?"

Anger flared in Johanna's chest. *How could Roland betray her by spreading such gossip? By telling an outright untruth?* "No," she said. "That's not the way it happened. *I* asked Roland to marry me, and *he* refused."

"Verhuddelt." Ruth shook her head. "I thought it was *lecherich*—ridiculous—but you know Dorcas. I thought it was best to ask you to your face. By now Aunt Martha has probably spread the rumor over half the county."

"And all the way up to Lancaster. By next week, they'll be talking about it in Oregon." Johanna felt sick. *What could make Roland say such a thing?*

Was he so ashamed of his reaction to her proposal that he had to make it seem as if everything was her fault? "If Roland's that low to spread such gossip, maybe it's better that he did refuse me."

"I've hurt you," Ruth said. "I didn't mean to. But I thought it best you hear it from family, rather than at church or at the market. And I won't ask you what happened. You can tell me when you're ready. If you want to tell me at all."

Johanna wasn't up for retelling the whole story, at least not right now. "Did Dorcas say where her mother heard it?"

"I think she said it came from Roland and Charley's sister Mary, but…" Ruth looked heavenward. "Dorcas never gets anything right. It could have been Rebecca or Miriam or even Anna. Roland is close to Charley. They confide in each other, and Charley can't keep anything from Miriam." She chuckled. "He's mad for her. You'd think they were still courting, rather than an old married couple."

"Aunt Ruth?" Katy peered through the open door to the porch. "Why can't the *bussli* open its eyes?"

"The light is too bright for such a young kitten. All in God's time, precious. Have you decided which one you want?"

"The black one with the white mittens. I'm going to call her Mittens."

Ruth laughed. "Mittens is a good name, but it isn't a girl. The black *bussli* is a boy."

Johanna stood up, grateful that Katy had interrupted their conversation. She didn't want to think about Roland or the stupid rumor that he'd started. She wanted to clean something. She wanted to scrub floors and wash windows, anything requiring physical effort…anything to stop the hurt gathering in the hollow place inside her. "Time I got to work," she said lightly. "Shall I start on this porch? I think the floor needs a good scrubbing."

Two hours, three floors and nine windows later, Johanna's temper flared just as hot. She knew she should just let it go, but she couldn't. She just couldn't.

"Would you watch Katy for me?" she asked Ruth. "I'm going over to Roland's and straighten this out with him."

"Now?" Ruth asked. "Of course. You know I love having Katy anytime." She grimaced. "I don't think I'd want to be Roland Byler just now."

"I'm not going to argue with him. I just want to know if he did tell anyone that I was the one who rejected him and why he did it—if it's true. I wouldn't want to jump to conclusions. Just because Dorcas said it, doesn't mean that it's so."

Ruth stirred sugar into her pitcher of iced tea.

"It's probably right that you two have this out now. But…"

"But what?"

Ruth grimaced. "Don't do or say anything that will make things worse."

"What could possibly make things worse? I made a fool out of myself by asking a man to marry me, and now the story, or at least *a* story, is spreading. I'll be a laughingstock, and so will my family."

Ruth hugged her. "I'm so sorry, Johanna. I'll admit, I wanted you and Roland to marry. I thought he'd be perfect for you."

So did I, Johanna thought. *So did I. But it's clear that I was badly mistaken.*

Roland drove the ax deep into the upright section of log and it split with a satisfying crack. He'd been at it since before noon, and the woodpile beside the corncrib was growing steadily. This was applewood, rescued from an English neighbor who had planned on having a bonfire after he cleared an old orchard. Apple burned clean and hot and gave off a wonderful smell. Burning applewood as trash was a terrible waste, but when he'd offered to buy the uprooted trees, Paul had suggested a trade. Two days' labor at harvest time in exchange for the applewood, an offer that Roland had been more than willing to accept.

There was an old saying, "Firewood heats twice, once when you chop it, and again when you burn it." That was true enough, but he'd be glad to have the cured logs when cold weather came. And splitting wood took a lot of effort. It kept a man's body in good shape, and prevented him from thinking too much about things that troubled him. At least, he'd hoped it might. Johanna had been worrying him like a stone wedged under a horse's shoe.

He couldn't help going over and over that last conversation they'd had at the Mennonite festival, when she'd suggested they marry, saying it as plainly as if she had asked him to pass the salt—and with as little emotion.

When he'd lost Pauline and the babes she was carrying, he'd felt for months as if he was dead inside. But then, when Johanna's husband had passed away, a small seed of hope had begun to sprout. Maybe there was a chance that he and Johanna could find what they'd both felt for each other once, and nourish it again. Maybe they could have a second chance.

Years ago, when Johanna had thrown him over, she'd been right to do it. He wasn't worthy of her, wasn't the man his mother and father had raised him to be. He'd paid the penalty for his reckless behavior. But later, he'd truly repented for his acts, and he'd returned to his faith. He'd been honest with Pauline, and she'd been willing to believe in him. He would have loved her for that, if for nothing else.

But when he began to live again, when his mourning for Pauline had grown bearable, he began to long for Johanna Yoder. He'd pictured her at his table, in his garden and in his orchard. He'd imagined walking to church with her and watching her face when she sang the old hymns. But in that dream, she loved him as much as he loved her. And if she didn't love him…if she couldn't, how could he go through with a farce? How could he marry a woman who wanted him because he had a good sheep meadow and a farm without a mortgage? Better to live alone than live a lie.… So why did it ache so much?

"Roland?"

He sank the blade of the ax into the chopping block and turned, expecting to see his sister Mary. She'd taken J.J. for the morning and promised to bring him back on her way to her afternoon cleaning job at an Englishwoman's house. But it wasn't Mary, and it wasn't J.J. Roland's pulse quickened at the sight of Johanna walking toward him.

"We need to talk," she said.

Chapter Seven

Roland stepped away from the woodpile, pulled off his leather work gloves and inhaled deeply. He was filthy and sweating heavily, no fit sight for a woman he'd hoped to court. But here she was and here he was, and it was face her or run, and he'd never been a coward.

"I'm listening," Roland said. His chest tightened, and he felt as if the earth was unsteady under his feet. Why was it that Johanna always made him feel unsure of himself? It wasn't just that her big blue eyes radiated strength, and it wasn't the unusual color of her red-gold hair, or her beautiful, heart-shaped face. A man would have to be blind not to see the neat waist or her tidy figure. But Johanna was a woman who had more that just beauty.

For him, she had always brought joy into his life. When he caught sight of her, his heart always beat a little faster and the sky seemed bluer. Johanna wasn't shy and retiring, like so many Amish girls, and she never hesitated to speak her mind. She didn't say the first thing that popped into her head, though, and she had a dry sense of humor that matched his own.

"Roland?" The sound of her voice was as soothing as rain on a tin roof after a drought.

He straightened his shoulders, shaking off the ache of hard-used muscles and the cramping at the back of his neck that came from swinging an ax for hours on end. "I'm sorry for the way we parted last," he said with what he hoped was quiet dignity.

"Did you tell anyone about what passed between us on Saturday?" Her tone came firm, without being strident, and her bright blue eyes demanded honesty.

Regret flooded him. Charley had a big mouth, and from the look on Johanna's face he'd obviously shared their conversation, at the very least with his wife. "I did," Roland admitted, trying not to sound defensive. "It troubled me that you and I should argue over something so important as marriage. I talked it out with my brother."

"I see." Johanna's lower lip trembled, and her face paled so that her freckles stood out against her creamy skin. She looked as if she might cry.

Roland swallowed. He never could abide a

woman's tears, and the thought that he might hurt Johanna enough to make her weep hit him like a horse's kick to his midsection.

She came closer and lowered her voice, although there was no one but God and the two of them to hear. "I ask because there's talk. Yesterday, Dorcas told my sister Ruth that you asked me to marry you and I wouldn't have you."

"What?" He blinked. "I never said that. I told Charley… I didn't repeat everything that passed between us, but I would never lie. I told Charley that it was me who said no."

"So Dorcas had it wrong?"

He nodded. "Dorcas had it wrong."

Johanna took a deep breath and glanced away, them back at him. "I'm glad." She looked… She looked vulnerable, and that made him feel even worse. He'd always thought of her as tough…but she wasn't. Not really. She just did a good job of hiding her weaknesses.

She took a step closer. "Despite our quarrel, Roland, I never thought you'd be one to go behind my back with an untruth. I thought it fair to come and ask you, face-to-face—not to just believe rumors."

"I appreciate that."

She nibbled at her bottom lip, and he saw that she was as nervous as he was. "But you told Charley."

He nodded. "I did. I thought I needed advice."

"And what did Charley say?"

Roland shrugged. "That the community…the family…think we should marry. They expect us to come to an agreement."

Johanna took another step toward him. Roland felt like a weather vane on top of a barn, gusts of wind catching it and blowing it first one way and then the other.

"And…do you still feel the same as when we talked last?" she asked. "About wanting romantic love? You don't think we should listen to those who know us best—if we shouldn't just make the match…for the sake of our children?"

He hesitated. This was his opportunity to make everything right. All he had to do was swallow his pride. He could have Johanna as his wife, as long as he didn't ask for her pledge of love. But he couldn't do it, because there could be no real marriage between a man and woman without honesty. "I do," he said. "My thoughts on that haven't changed."

"All right," she agreed. "That's fair. I still stand by my words, as well."

Disappointment made him bold. Or maybe it was the thread of hope he still held in his heart. "Is it because of what happened between us when we were walking out?" he asked. "How I failed you? Or is the problem because of Wilmer?"

She looked unsure. Maybe a little afraid. Not

of him…but of herself. "I don't know," she said. "Maybe both."

He knew how close he was to pushing too far with this honesty, but he had to take the chance. "And is this something that could change, or is there no chance of…of love between us?"

She covered her mouth with that slender hand and shook her head. Slowly, she lowered her hand. "I don't know, Roland."

He exhaled, letting out a breath he hadn't realized he had been holding. Did she mean there *was* a chance?

"We're agreed, then," she said. "The question is, what do we do about the gossip?"

Agreed? There had been no agreement. They were like two hardheaded goats with their horns locked together. "Why do we have to do anything? It's what we know that matters. Next week they'll be talking about somebody else."

"It *does* matter," Johanna said. "These are our friends, our neighbors…our family. How did the story get twisted from what you told Charley to what Dorcas told Ruth?"

"I'm sure you have more important things to worry about than what Dorcas says."

"So I'm to go to each person who's heard this tale and straighten them out?"

He shrugged. "I'd let it lie. If you talk to Ruth,

she'll tell Eli and Miriam. Miriam will tell Charley and—"

"I thought Charley had it straight."

"He did, from me." Roland flushed. "I suppose, I shouldn't have said anything to him but—"

"*Ne.* You shouldn't have. It wasn't Charley's business. It was private, between us." Her mouth firmed. "I wish you'd left it that way."

"So I shouldn't talk to my brother about what's bothering me, but it's all right for you to share what passes between us with your sisters?"

She folded her arms. "I didn't come here to argue with you, Roland."

"I suppose I should be grateful for that."

"You should." She looked down at her bare feet and surprised him with a chuckle. "Listen to us, arguing like an old married couple. "I'm sorry. I came to get an explanation, but I never doubted you. You can be thickheaded, but you're…"

"A decent person?" He forced a wry smile. "While you're here, you might as well tend your bees, and I'll finish chopping my wood. I think we've both said enough on this subject to last a week or two."

"If it bothers you, my coming here to look after the hive, I can move it. I think they're settled enough now. If I come at night and—"

"Keep your bees here as long as you like. They're no trouble to me, and it seems they like my garden. I see them everywhere. Even I know that it's safer to move them in cool weather. I wouldn't want to see you lose them after all your hard work."

She nodded. "There's sense in that. But I'll tell you plainly, I mean to find out what Charley said and who he said it to."

"That again, is it?" Roland shrugged again. "Go to it, if it pleases you, but I'll have no part of your detective game." She turned to walk away, and he couldn't resist saying, "There's a work frolic at the Stutzman brothers'—you know the Lancaster Amish who bought the Englisher farm next to Norman and Lydia's. On Saturday the twenty-first. Not this Saturday but the following. Some of us are going to build a dog-proof pasture fence and a shed for their dairy-goat herd."

"Lydia said they were camping in a tent on the property, but I haven't met them."

"Thomas and Will Stutzman, brothers. Big lot of their friends and family coming down from Pennsylvania in July to put up a house, but they needed help to get their herd settled in."

Johanna relaxed her arms and tilted her head, obviously curious. "*Mam* said that she'd heard they were cheese makers."

"It's mostly young married couples and those walking out going. Charley and Miriam are going, and so are Mary and Little Joe King. We're having food and a bonfire after dark. Maybe you'd like to come with me?"

She hesitated. "I don't think so. Not with things the way they stand with us."

"So this time, you're refusing me," he said quietly.

"I'm afraid so." She averted her eyes. "I don't mind going to help out our new neighbors, but I'll drive myself or come with Charley and Miriam. There's no sense in causing more talk about us.... Or in pretending we're courting, when we're not."

"We wouldn't want that," he said, trying to keep the edge from his voice. "Especially since there's no *us* to feed the gossip."

The following afternoon, Johanna, Jonah and 'Kota were driving Johanna's flock of sheep from one pasture into the low meadow with the aid of *Mam's* Shetland sheepdog Flora. Nine of the cheviot ewes and their lambs were obediently following the dominant cheviot ewe, but two didn't want to cooperate. The troublemaker, as usual, was Snowball—the only Cormo. She managed to squeeze under the fence, followed by a straggler, and trot toward the cornfield.

"Abatz dummkopf!" 'Kota cried, pointing at the escapees. "Stop, stupid heads!"

"They're going into the corn!" Jonah shouted.

"You two keep the flock moving toward the

meadow, and when they're all in, close the gate. But wait there until I chase the other two back, and let them in."

"And lock the gate!" 'Kota jumped from one foot to the other with excitement.

Since he'd come to live at *Mam's* farm last fall, he'd fallen in love with barnyard animals, but the sheep were his favorite. He was fascinated by every aspect of caring for them, including the lambing and the shearing of their fleece. Jonah, in contrast, liked the sheep well enough, but he favored the larger animals. He loved nothing more than trailing after his uncle Charley and helping to tend the horses and cows.

Johanna hitched up her skirt and climbed over the fence. The two sheep had found a row of corn and were busily munching on the six-inch-high plants. "Shoo! Shoo!" Johanna said.

Charley came out of the orchard on a three-year-old gelding that he was breaking to saddle for an Englishwoman and spotted the runaway sheep. He shouted to Johanna. "I'll give you a hand!"

She waved her apron and ran at the two sheep. The cheviot ewe went one way, and Snowball went in the opposite direction, a mouthful of corn leaves dangling from her mouth. Johanna took off after Snowball, leaving the other ewe for Charlie to corral.

The silly creature trotted down the rows of corn

just as Aunt Martha and *Mam* came into the yard in her husband's, Uncle Reuben's, buggy. The two women climbed down and made an attempt to chase Snowball into an open shed. Hearing the shouting, Susanna and Rebecca left the side yard, where they'd been hanging clothes, and joined in the pursuit. Susanna caught hold of Snowball's collar, but the sheep yanked free and made for the garden gate with Aunt Martha and *Mam* hot on the animal's heels.

Johanna tripped over a clod of dirt and fell on her bottom. Then she began to laugh. Seeing her mother and Aunt Martha running after the ewe was the funniest thing she'd seen in weeks. She laughed until she was breathless and tears of laughter ran down her cheeks. She was still laughing when Charley rode up on the gelding.

"I got mine," he said. "Chased it back through the fence. The boys turned it in with the others."

"I didn't get mine," she admitted between chuckles. "For all I know, it's halfway to Dover. That one sheep is more trouble than the whole flock." She got to her feet and brushed the dirt off her hands and skirt.

Charley took off his hat and wiped the sweat off his forehead. The horse danced nervously and twitched its ears. Charley stroked the animal's neck and spoke soothingly to it. "Easy, easy, boy."

He looked back at her. "If it's so much trouble, why keep it? Send it to the sale."

Johanna sighed. "Snowball doesn't belong to me. Wilmer brought it home for Katy, just before he died. The man he worked for couldn't pay his wages and gave Wilmer the ewe instead. She's worth a lot of money. She's a Cormo, and their wool is greatly sought after. I hoped to improve my flock with her and we could always use the extra money."

"And meanwhile, you put up with the monster."

"I suppose I do." She rolled her eyes. "Aunt Martha may have killed her by now. She nearly ran Aunt Martha and *Mam* over, and I think they chased her through the garden."

Charley tugged his hat down. "Sorry I missed that."

"Me, too." She surveyed the damaged corn. "At least they didn't have time to eat enough to make themselves sick or to destroy too much of the crop."

"The flock could do some damage here," Charley remarked.

Johanna nodded. *Mam* was coming to depend more and more on him to do the heavy farming. With the girls marrying off, one by one, it was a blessing that they had Charley and that he and Miriam would continue to work *Dat's* land in the future.

He shifted in the saddle. "You and my brother still butting heads?"

Johanna frowned. "I've been wanting to talk to you. I understand that Roland told you about something that happened between us—that I said it made sense for us to marry. And he turned me down. Is that what he said?"

Charley nodded. "That's what he said."

"Well, there's a rumor going around. And it seems people have it all wrong. What did you tell Miriam?"

Charley's brow wrinkled. "Nothing. I didn't say anything to her. I thought that you'd tell her yourself—if you wanted her to know."

Johanna gazed up at him. "But if you didn't tell Miriam, who did you tell?"

Charley's face reddened. "Mary. I didn't mean to. It just slipped out. She was asking about Roland, and…"

"Did you tell anyone else that he'd refused to marry me?"

"Ne." Charley shook his head. "Nobody. Just Mary."

"So I'll have to find out who Mary confided in, because Ruth heard a completely different story from Dorcas. Her mother told her that I didn't want to marry Roland." Johanna grimaced. "Now the neighborhood is talking about us, and they don't even have the story right."

"I'm sorry, Johanna. I feel awful. I should have kept my mouth shut." The horse pawed the ground, and Charley reined him in a tight circle. "Hope you aren't too mad at me."

Johanna shook her head. "No, not mad. Of course, if Roland hadn't said anything to you, none of this would have happened."

He sat there for a moment. "Oh, Miriam wanted me to ask you if you wanted to go fishing with us on Saturday. We bought tickets to go out on a charter boat in the Delaware Bay. For trout. Eli was going to go, but now he can't. Miriam knows how much you like fishing, and Eli's giving away the ticket. Anna said she'd be glad to watch Katy and Jonah for you."

"I haven't been fishing in the bay for years, not since Katy was born. I'd like that."

"We've got a driver. Be ready at five. And pack a big lunch. They have water and soft drinks on the boat."

Johanna heard someone call her name and turned to see *Mam* and Aunt Martha coming toward her, dragging Snowball behind them on a length of clothesline. "Did you lose something?" *Mam* asked.

"You caught her. I hope she didn't tear up too much of the garden."

"No sheep born that can get away from me,"

Aunt Martha proclaimed proudly. "You've just got to show an animal who's boss."

It was all Johanna could do to not start laughing again. Aunt Martha had dirt and bits of wool stuck to the front of her dress and apron. Her shoes were caked with dirt, her *Kapp* was wrinkled and nearly falling off the back of her head, and there was a big smudge on her cheek and another on her nose.

Charley choked and began coughing, said a hasty goodbye and rode off, leaving Johanna struggling to maintain her dignity.

"I almost had her in the lettuce," *Mam* said, "but she broke loose and ran through the beans. I don't know where she'd be if Martha hadn't dove on her back and rode her to a standstill."

Johanna's eyes widened. "You did that, Aunt Martha?"

Aunt Martha nodded vigorously. "That beast deserves nothing better than to be carved up and served with new potatoes and baby beets. She's a danger to life and limb."

Mam's smile spread across her face and her eyes twinkled. "You're just lucky that Martha was here when you needed her, Johanna," she said. "Otherwise, it would have been a real disaster."

Aunt Martha beamed. "I always did have a hand with sheep," she boasted as she glanced at

Mam and began to chuckle. "And just between us women, I haven't had so much fun in a month of Sundays."

Chapter Eight

Ribbons of lavender and peach uncoiled on the eastern horizon as Johanna, Miriam, Charley and three other Amish men climbed onto the deck of the charter boat *Gone Fishin' IV.* Overhead, Johanna heard the screech of seagulls and, below, the lap of gray-green waves against the weathered dock. The tangy air smelled of salt marsh and bay, and even though it was early, the night dampness was already evaporating from the shore, leaving a promise of a glorious day.

Bowers Beach, the small bayside fishing village, teemed with pickup trucks and boat trailers. Excited sportsmen and commercial fishermen rushed to stock up on bait and ice and launch their vessels. Off the stern of the charter boat, seemingly oblivious to the commotion, a mallard hen bobbed on the choppy waves, trailed by seven tiny yellow-and-brown ducklings. Gulls shrieked and dove for scraps in the shallows, and Johanna caught sight of a huge horseshoe crab lurking in the shadows of the dock. She leaned so far over the gunnel to watch it that, for a moment, she struggled to keep her balance. Then, out of nowhere, someone snatched her back from the edge of the boat.

"Careful," a familiar male voice warned. "Don't want to have you fall overboard. That water's too cold to suit me, and I'd have to dive in and pull you out."

Johanna's eyes widened in surprise as she turned to him. "Roland! What are you doing here?" She took a step back from him, planting her hand on her hip. "And, if you recall, the last time one of us fell into the pond, *I* had to rescue *you*."

A shy grin lifted the corners of his mouth and added sparkle to his eyes. "I was nine, and I didn't know how to swim yet."

"I was younger than you, but my *dat* made certain his girls all knew how to swim."

Roland grimaced. "You're never going to let me forget that, are you?"

Johanna turned away, glancing at the water. There was no way this was coincidence, she and Roland being on the same charter boat. It had to be a plot cooked up by her sister and brother-in-law, but Roland was obviously in on it, too. She supposed that she should be angry, but she couldn't help finding it just a little funny. The horseshoe crab she'd been watching had vanished into the dark depths under the dock.

One of the reasons she'd agreed to come on this fishing trip was to get away from thinking about Roland, and trying to explain to family and friends what had and hadn't happened between them. But instead of leaving her trouble back at Seven Poplars, she was trapped on this fishing boat with him for the entire day.

Can't run away from stuff you fear, Johanna heard her father whisper from the shadows of her mind. *Be it a rotten tooth or a bad mule, may as well face it down,* he'd always advised. And *Dat* was right. She couldn't run from Roland…didn't know if she wanted to. That was the trouble…she didn't know what she wanted, and just being near him made her common sense fly out the window.

"You didn't answer my question," she said, turning back to Roland. "What are you doing here?"

"I'm on this boat to catch fish—same as you."

What Roland said was mild enough, but the expression on his face—when she turned to face him—was smug. And they both knew that fishing wasn't his entire reason for being there.

For just an instant, she had the most wicked urge to give him a good shove overboard. She imagined what a big splash he would make. But she couldn't do that, no matter how much satisfaction it might give her. Charley and Miriam were probably watching, waiting to see what she would do. They were hoping for a show, and she was determined not to give them one.

It was too late to chicken out and just go home. The captain had already started the boat's engines, and they were pulling away from the dock. Besides, the driver who'd brought them in his van had already left, and wouldn't return until five o'clock. She would have to deal with Roland, no matter what his ulterior motive. She had come here to go fishing. She wouldn't let Roland ruin her day.

After a moment's thought, she offered her hand. "Truce?"

He returned her smile and shook on it. "As I said, just wanted to go fishing."

Why did she doubt that? And why did the sight of him, standing there, so tall and appealing, make her heart beat just a little faster? *You're too old for this nonsense,* she told herself. Her head had been filled with ideas of romance once, and life had taught her differently. But why did her hand tingle from the touch of his? And why did her chest tighten and her stomach feel as if she'd swallowed a handful of goose down?

"And maybe I came so I could see you," he admitted. "Just as a bonus."

She leaned against the cabin, enjoying the feel of the boat rocking gently under her. "I thought we'd agreed that this was a mistake…looking for a match between us."

His eyes were shaded under the brim of his straw hat. Oddly, it disappointed her that she couldn't see the expression in them. Roland had never been good at hiding from her what he was thinking. He didn't answer.

"Whose idea was it for you to come?" she asked softly. She wondered what had ever possessed her to propose marriage to Roland in the first place. That was what had caused all this upset. It would have been better for her and Roland both if she had just let things remain as they were, rather than stirring up feelings from long ago.

Her life with *Mam,* her children, her sisters and her faith were all fine just the way they were. Seeking out Roland had been a mistake that just made things more complicated. "Whose idea was it," she repeated, "for you to come on the boat and not tell me?"

"Charley's."

Johanna's eyes narrowed. "And Miriam's? She had to be in on it." Wait until she got her sister alone. She'd give her a good piece of her mind. Johanna sighed. "Nothing has changed, Roland," she said. She looked up at him again. "But we used to be friends…a long time ago. Maybe we could just be friends again…for today."

He stepped close to her, steady despite the rocking of the boat as it sliced through the waves. "You know I want to be more than friends, Johanna."

She folded her arms over her chest. "If we're going to have a truce today, you have to promise not to talk about that anymore."

"You're tough," he murmured, switching to Pennsylvania Dutch.

"Tough enough to catch more fish than you," she answered in the same dialect.

"I guess we'll just have to see about that." He didn't move away, and they stood there, watching as the dock grew smaller and smaller in the wake of the *Gone Fishin' IV*.

Three middle-aged Amish men from one of the other church districts had taken spots on the deck a few yards away. She knew them by name, but not well. One man owned a greenhouse, and the other two, she thought, worked as masons. Johanna couldn't see her sister or Charley. They were probably hiding out on the other side of the boat, as well they should.

A black-and-white osprey soared overhead on powerful wings, with a fish caught in its talons. She watched it until the beautiful bird was out of sight. Already, the sky was growing much brighter, and the rising sun painted a wide swath of the rippling water orange-gold. Other boats passed them, motors roaring, and a buoy bobbed as the *Gone Fishin's* captain went around it. A family on a pontoon boat in the distance had already anchored, and Johanna could see a boy Jonah's age lowering a crab line over the side while a woman dipped a long-handled net into the waves.

Johanna stared at the churning surface of the water, inhaling deeply. She'd always loved the smell of the salt air. It took her back to all the times *Dat* had taken them fishing, crabbing and wading in the ocean when she was a child. They'd gone every summer since she'd been born…until he died. Her father had been a good swimmer, and he'd taught them all to swim, including *Mam* and Susanna. Susanna was still awkward, but she'd become an expert at floating and could keep her head above water as well as any of them.

It had been important to *Dat* that they all learned to swim because of a boating tragedy that happened when he was a teenager. An Amish youth group had gone out on an excursion boat somewhere on one of the Great Lakes. There had been an accident, and the boat had gone down, taking far too many of the children with it because none of them could swim. *Dat* had promised himself that it would never happen to his family, if he could prevent it. *Have faith in God,* he would say. *But God doesn't expect us to be foolish servants*.

It hit Johanna that her father would be upset with her if he knew that she hadn't yet taught Katy and Jonah to swim. This summer, she'd have to do something about that.

Wilmer hadn't been able to swim a lick, and he had forbidden her to teach their children. He hadn't liked boats or the beach, and he had never eaten fish or seafood of any kind. It troubled Johanna that her own little ones had missed the joys of hunting for seashells, digging clams and watching long-legged water birds foraging in the marsh grass. Wilmer had forbidden her to even wade in the water, saying that it wasn't decent for a woman.

But Wilmer was gone. She couldn't use him as an excuse for neglecting her children's safety anymore. She was the one to decide what was best for her children. "Have you taught J.J. to swim?" she asked Roland.

He nodded solemnly. "I have. I wasn't satisfied until he could jump into our pond fully clothed with his shoes on and swim from one end to the other."

She considered that. "Maybe," she ventured, "if it wouldn't be too much trouble, you could find time to teach my Jonah this summer."

"I would be pleased to," Roland said. "And what of Katy?"

"*Ne*," she said. "You know how shy she is. I can give her lessons myself." Roland wasn't her father…wasn't her uncle or brother. It wouldn't be fitting for her to ask him to perform such an intimate thing for her little girl. Of course he could, she thought. If they married and Roland became her children's father. If only things weren't so complicated between them.

Maybe Roland wasn't really the problem. Maybe the problem was her. Maybe it was the thought of giving herself and her children over to any man that frightened her. Was that why she told him she could never love him?

Among the Old Order Amish, the man was the head of the family and his was the final say. He could decide to leave one church group and attend another, and his wife would have to do as he wished. Roland, or any husband she might choose, could—if he wished—move them to Wisconsin or Colorado or even to Canada, as some of the faith had done. A husband would have the right and the power to turn her life upside down, and there would be nothing she could do or say to prevent it…nothing but remain single.

Maybe she was too attached to her mother and her sisters…. But the truth was, she still didn't want to leave Seven Poplars…she still needed her family around her. And to do that…to make certain that her life remained as it was, she would have to remain single, like her mother.

It was so much safer this way. Immediately, relief flooded through her. She didn't have to chance their future. She could keep things just as they were until her children were grown. It wasn't as if she didn't have a home, didn't have a place to raise Katy and Jonah. She had her bees and her sheep and her quilts. Her desire for a baby would pass, wouldn't it? She didn't need a man…not really. And she didn't need Roland.

Well…maybe she did, but as a friend…as they had been when they were children. She'd thought of Roland then as a brother or maybe a cousin. It wasn't until things changed…until she'd allowed him to take her home from frolics and singings that he'd become something more. It wasn't until they'd walked out together and she'd allowed him to hold her hand when they walked through the orchard that she'd begun to think of what it would be like to be his wife.

She and Roland had shared a time of fun and laughter and dreams…until he had betrayed her and everything had gone wrong between them. Then she'd married Wilmer, on impulse for certain.

She'd thought she was so grown-up when she and Wilmer had taken their vows before God and Bishop Atlee, when they'd sat at the bride and groom's table with family and friends around them. But she'd had so much to learn. She'd not always been wise and she'd not always had charity in her heart for Wilmer's weaknesses. But she'd never realized just how lost he was…until it was too late.

"Johanna, look!"

Roland's words brought her back to the present and she glanced in the direction he pointed. A smooth, dark head cut the water, and as she watched, a beautiful bottlenose dolphin dove out of the water, followed by a second, a third and a fourth.

"One of God's wonders," Roland remarked.

Johanna exhaled softly, caught in the excitement of the moment as the dolphins raced beside the boat, diving and leaping and diving again, seemingly just for the joy of being alive. *I wish I'd brought Jonah with me. Maybe if Roland teaches him to swim, I can take him on a fishing boat next year. Jonah would love to see the dolphins and the other boats and the seabirds, and he would love trying to catch fish.* Katy was too young to come out on the bay yet, but someday, Johanna promised herself, someday, she would bring Katy, too.

"I've got a bite!" Johanna called.

Another one? Roland bit back the words. It was mean-spirited to resent Johanna's prowess, and he didn't really feel that way. Still, in the hour since the captain had anchored at Fourteen Foot Lighthouse, Johanna had already caught a nice-size trout and a croaker. The only thing that he'd managed to land was one toadfish and a sea bass too small to keep.

Charley had three trout, and Miriam had caught a flounder. If things didn't improve, Johanna would never let him hear the end of it. It wasn't that he was a terrible fisherman. He was using the same bait as everyone else, and he was just as capable of catching fish. The trouble was, nothing was biting on his hook.

But his day wasn't all bad. Johanna was actually speaking to him, and they were having a good time. Once she'd gotten over her annoyance that they were spending the day together, she'd begun to act more like her old self. It was good to see her laugh. They'd always found things to talk about, and today was no exception. Johanna never hesitated to give her opinion, but she wasn't one of those women who always had to dominate the conversation. She was a good listener, and when she listened to him, he felt as if she really paid attention to what he said.

Roland kept coming back to the same conclusion—that if he and Johanna ever could work out their differences, she would make a good partner. She was the kind of woman who could hold up her end of the marriage, a strong woman, a woman who wouldn't fall to pieces if misfortune came. She was the kind of woman he was looking for.

He'd loved Pauline; he really had. She'd been

a good wife, but her poor health had often made her sad or worried. She'd become fearful for J.J. in the last year before her death, so much so that at times they knocked heads over what was best for the boy. She'd wanted to protect J.J. so badly that Roland often felt shut out of his own son's life. Still, Pauline's passing had hit them both hard. Never a night did he lay his head on the pillow to sleep that he didn't remember to pray for her, and to hope that she and the children that she'd miscarried were safe in God's care.

But Pauline was in heaven and he was here. A decent time had passed since her death, and he'd felt that it was time to move on with his life...time to give J.J. a new mother and time for him to have a wife and, God willing, more children. He wanted Johanna Yoder to be that wife. He couldn't picture any other woman walking beside him in the garden or sitting across the supper table and sharing evening grace. He could see Johanna there, her sweet heart-shaped face, those wide blue eyes so full of wisdom, and the soft curve of her mouth when she smiled.

Was it so wrong of him to want her to love him? To want to put the mistakes he'd made in the past? To want more than an arranged marriage as his parents' had been? His *mam* and *dat* respected each other and worked well together. He could never remember his mother raising her voice in anger to his father. They had reared three children and buried two more. *Dat's* farm was a well-maintained one, and the family had never suffered real want. His parents were faithful to church and were good neighbors, never ones to cause trouble or dissension in the community. But Roland had never felt that there was a powerful man's and woman's love between his mother and father. And, selfishly, he wanted that. He wanted Johanna to love him so badly that if she couldn't, he was pretty sure he would walk away.

But was he thinking wrongly? According to the way he'd been raised, a marriage was supposed to be for family, for community, for carrying on God's work and raising children in the faith. A marriage was not to fulfill the selfish desires of a man and a woman, so a marriage of convenience was as good a way to form a family as a romantic attraction between couples. Young people were expected to listen to their parents and the elders of the church. Mature friends and relatives who knew the prospective couple were often in a better position to provide sound advice on the suitability of the match than the girl and boy themselves.

Roland couldn't accept that. Marriage was for life. If he didn't choose well, if he picked a woman he found difficult to live with, he wanted to be solely responsible. *Be honest.* He wanted desperately for Johanna Yoder to love him.

Another trout flopped wildly on the deck between him and Johanna. "You can have that one," she teased. "I wouldn't want you to go home without anything to cook for J.J.'s supper."

He chuckled. "Thanks, but the truth is, if I fried it, it wouldn't be fit for J.J. or me to eat."

The mate removed Johanna's fish from her hook and carried it to the fish box. "Maybe Cap'n should hire you to show the others how to catch fish," he said.

Johanna laughed and glanced at Roland as the mate walked away. "You have an oven. Frying isn't the only way to cook fish. You could bake it, or even make a fish stew."

"But fried fish sounds good." Roland caught her line and carefully baited her hook with a fresh piece of squid. "*Mam* always served it with johnnycake or corn bread. Maybe you could come over and cook it for me."

She arched an eyebrow. "And why would I want to do that?"

"Charity." He thrust out his upper lip, pretending to look forlorn. "Pity on a poor widower who needs a decent meal. And his young, undernourished son," he added.

She tried not to smile, but she couldn't help herself. "Roland. I don't think my making suppers for you is such a good—"

"Truce, right?"

She was laughing now. *"Ya,"* she agreed.

"And we're friends again?" he urged.

"Ya, I suppose we are friends."

"Then, as a friend, I could ask you to cook for me the fish that you have so graciously offered to share."

She cast her baited line over the edge of the boat, and the lead sinker pulled it down. She kept her eyes on the line where it disappeared into the water, but he knew he had her attention.

"Come on, Johanna." He could tell by the look on her face that she was about to give in. "There's nothing wrong with friends sharing a meal, is there? And three children should be chaperone enough to spare either of our reputations."

"Maybe I could whip you up some fried fish tonight," she said. "It wouldn't take long to make."

"I've got cornmeal."

"I'd need flour and shortening and milk."

"Got them."

"And we'd have to pick up my children first. I'll not come to your house alone and be the subject of loose talk."

"Fair enough," he said.

The tip of her fishing pole dipped. She let it go, then yanked back hard when it dipped again. The resulting tug was so hard that she nearly lost her balance. Roland dropped his own pole, threw his arms around her and gripped her fishing rod. There was a fierce pull and then the line snapped.

Roland stood where he was, holding Johanna in his arms for a few seconds. "Roland!" she protested. From somewhere, he heard Charley's laughter.

"Sorry." Reluctantly, Roland released her. "I was afraid that fish might pull you in."

She gave him a look as if he was up to no good, but she was onto him. "I doubt that."

"It was huge. Might have been anything. A shark—even a whale."

"A whale?" She began to laugh. "You're impossible."

He laughed with her, and it felt good to be standing on the deck of a rocking boat in the June sunshine, but not nearly as good as holding her for that brief scrap of time.

Chapter Nine

By the time Johanna and the others arrived home from the fishing trip, it was too late to bring her children to Roland's farm for a fish supper. They'd had a busy day and were already sitting down to a cold supper. Instead, when her mother offered to keep Katy and Jonah, Johanna invited Susanna and Aunt Jezzy to come as chaperones. It was a good decision because it was after eight o'clock when Johanna and Susanna got the promised meal on Roland's table.

Aunt Jezzy contributed her famous wild dandelion and lettuce salad, rich with hard-cooked eggs and Swiss cheese, and a loaf of her delicious potato sponge bread. All Johanna had to do was roll the fish filets in egg, flour and cornmeal and fry to a golden brown. *Mam* sent along a Dutch apple tart for a sweet, and Susanna's contribution was a plate of anise cookies that she'd baked that afternoon.

"I made them for King David," Susanna said, proudly showing Johanna the plate of cookies as they set the food on the table. "Me. For King David. For after church. But you…you can have some."

"They look wonderful," Johanna said as she set the platter of crispy fish on the table with the other dishes.

Roland and his sister Mary came downstairs from tucking J.J. into bed and joined them in the kitchen. Mary had spent the day with J.J. and had given him his supper earlier. She would be sharing the fish fry with them.

Mary lived with her and Roland's parents about four miles away in another church district, one that held Sunday services on a different schedule than the Seven Poplars community. Since tomorrow was a Visiting Sunday for her, Charley had invited her to spend the night and attend church service in Seven Poplars. Afterward, he could drive her home in his buggy.

When Mary protested that she hadn't brought her Sunday-go-to-church dress and bonnet, Johanna assured her that she could loan her something suitable. So, instead of spending the night with Roland, it was arranged that Mary would sleep over at the Yoder farm.

Johanna was pleased. She and Mary had been friends since they were children, and she knew her whole family would enjoy visiting with her. Besides, Johanna welcomed the opportunity to get Mary alone so that she could ask her exactly what Charley had told her about Roland's refusal to marry her. Johanna also was eager to find out to whom Mary had passed on the tale.

Roland had made it clear that he didn't care what other people might believe, but it mattered to Johanna, and she wouldn't be satisfied until she tracked the false gossip to its source. She didn't believe for a moment that Roland would be dishonest about what he told Charley, but she would feel better once she found out who had become confused and was spreading false information about her.

Everyone gathered at Roland's table and lowered their heads for silent grace. Johanna had to remind herself that these sacred moments were for being thankful to God for his blessings, not for remembering how much fun she'd had today, or for wondering if the fish had cooked through. Frying fish was an art. She had her own secret for the coating, but if the fish was overdone, it would be a shame.

Chastising herself for failing in grace, she allowed a quiet moment to flow through her, and her unspoken words of thankful praise poured out in truly heartfelt passion. She had so much to be grateful for, and those around her were a large part of her life—even Roland, as much as she hated to admit it.

"Johanna."

Susanna's merry voice cut through her thoughts. Johanna opened her eyes to see everyone looking at her expectantly.

Susanna's mouth puckered with impatience. "Can we eat *now?*" she begged. "I'm hungry… an' the fish…the fish smells so *gut.*"

"Of course." Johanna smiled in spite of her discomfort that she'd kept everyone waiting. *Dear, dear Susanna. Trust her to bring me back from my self-absorption.* Cheeks glowing with embarrassment, Johanna passed the heaping plate of fish to Roland. As he accepted the platter, their gazes met and warm pleasure made her want to giggle as lightheartedly as Susanna.

Aunt Jezzy passed the salad, and soon everyone was laughing and talking. There was something about Roland's house that made them all feel comfortable. It wasn't as large as *Mam's,* and the kitchen had lower ceilings and open chestnut beams overhead, but Johanna found it charming. *People have been happy here.*

And from deep inside came the disquieting thought, *Maybe I could be happy here, too.*

Johanna banished the wispy dream. Best to enjoy the moment…the evening of family and friends. With Mary, Susanna and Aunt Jezzy here, she quickly shed the awkwardness that being alone with Roland so often brought on. She could relax and be herself. And she could delight in Roland's exaggerated stories about the huge fish that bit on his line but somehow managed to escape after prolonged battles, fabrications that they all knew were just for fun.

To her delight, the fish was perfect, bursting with flavor, crunchy on the outside and succulent on the inside. The preachers taught that pride was contrary to plain living, but she couldn't help taking secret satisfaction from Roland's compliments on the supper.

He'd always made her laugh, and tonight was no exception. The friendship between them made conversation so easy and the meal so much fun. Johanna was just sorry that it had been too late in the day for Katy and Jonah to join them. It seemed strange not to have their sweet faces looking back at her across the table. Next time, she would make certain that all three children could share the meal with them. Next time…

Don't be foolish. Why would there be more suppers at Roland's house?

"What I want to know, Johanna," Roland said as he reached for another slice of Aunt Jezzy's sponge bread, "is how you caught so many more fish than me?" He made such a sad face that Susanna giggled. "We used the same bait and we were fishing in the same spot. What's your secret?"

Johanna chuckled. "You really want to know?" And when he nodded, she shrugged. "It's simple, Roland. Every time I bait my hook and drop it overboard, I pray."

"I didn't tell anyone but my mother that you and Roland had discussed marriage," Mary confided the next morning as she and Johanna walked down the farm lane to the main road. Katy and Jonah trailed behind them, chattering to each other. Roman and Fannie's chair shop, where church would be held today, stood at the intersection of Seven Poplars Road and School Lane, just down the street.

Mary lowered her voice. "And I told her what Roland told me…that he had not consented," she said, putting it delicately. "At least for now."

"I just can't understand it," Johanna said. She tried to focus on the purpose of the conversation and not the confusing emotions that kept popping up. "Somehow the story got turned around."

She and Mary wore identical dark blue dresses and aprons, black bonnets and black leather shoes. Small Katy's dress was a pale robin's-egg blue, but her prayer *Kapp* was white and her apron crackly-stiff with starch. Jonah wore a white shirt, black trousers and a black vest over his new high-top leather boots. His straw hat was new as well, because he'd outgrown his last hat. This one had just arrived Friday from the mail-order house where *Mam* had always purchased the items of clothing that they couldn't make.

"It was kind of your mother to lend me your sister's dress and bonnet," Mary said. "I've been wanting to attend your services. I should have thought to bring my good clothes when I came to watch J.J."

"*Ne.* It's no problem. With so many women in our house, there are always extra dresses," Johanna assured her.

Mary was closer to Leah's size than Johanna's, so *Mam* had fetched Leah's church dress out of her Old German marriage chest. "I know Leah wouldn't mind," Johanna continued. Since her sister had turned Mennonite and gone to Brazil as a missionary with her new husband, the dress had lain unused. *Mam* kept it carefully wrapped in tissue paper and sprinkled with dried basil and rosemary to ward off moths.

"But it was still nice of your *mam,*" Mary said. They walked on a little farther, waited until no cars were passing and crossed the road, the children still a few steps behind them. "About what you asked me before…about the talk. Maybe it's best to let it all drop."

"But I need to get to the bottom of this," Johanna said.

"No, you don't. You need to just let it go. It's not important."

Johanna's first impulse was to disagree, but she knew there was truth to what Mary was saying.

"The gossip about you and Roland will die down on its own," Mary suggested. "If you two aren't going to walk out together, word will get around."

Johanna knew that Mary was disappointed that things hadn't worked out between the two of them. She'd been as eager as Ruth and Anna for the match. *Roland's mother, Deborah, probably not as much.*

Deborah Byler had been born and raised in Kentucky in a very strict community and made it clear that she didn't approve of the Yoder girls—or of Widow Hannah Yoder, for that matter. *Mam's* choice to remain single and teach school instead of remarrying was still something of a scandal in the other Kent County church districts. Their own church community here in Seven Poplars and Bishop Atlee, thankfully, accepted *Mam* for the blessing she was.

When Charley and Miriam had been courting, Mary had told Johanna that their mother expressed doubt that Miriam was right for her son.

Apparently, Deborah was shocked at Miriam's doing fieldwork and seeing to the livestock, rather than tending to traditional women's chores in the house. In Deborah's opinion, all the Yoder women showed a lack of superior values and were altogether too headstrong to make proper wives. But *Mam* said that she would rather her girls be outspoken than to make judgments about people they'd never taken the effort to get to know.

"There's the bench wagon!" Jonah cried, pointing to a low, enclosed vehicle parked in the side yard of the chair shop. "Look, *Mam!* I helped Uncle Charley bring it from the Beachys'. He let me drive the team."

Johanna arched an eyebrow. "Uncle Charley let you drive? On the road?"

No family had enough chairs for the entire church. Instead, each community had their own collection of folding benches that they carried from house to house every two weeks. When Roman and Fannie hosted church, service was held in the large workshop, rather than in their home, because the house was too small to accommodate the congregation. The previous day, Charley, Eli, Roman and Irwin had cleaned the woodshop and set up the benches and chairs. Preparations for church were always done the previous day because no work could be done on Sunday. Johanna was pleased that Charley and Eli had thought to include Jonah. Without a father, it was important that he learn from other men how to be helpful.

Jonah's cheeks flushed cherry-red under his wide-brimmed straw hat. "*Ne.* I didn't really drive…but I held the reins," he added quickly. "And I helped Uncle Eli sweep the workshop, too."

"Irwin said you did," Johanna agreed. "He told me that you were a big help."

Jonah grinned. "I was."

"I hear Eli's a partner in Roman's chair shop now," Mary said as they drew closer to the chair shop.

Johanna nodded. "You probably know that it was my father who started the business. It did so well that he needed a partner, so he asked his friend Roman to move down from Pennsylvania. Roman hired Eli, and after Eli and Ruth married, *Mam* gave her interest in the chair shop to them as a wedding gift. It would please *Dat,* I know. Eli's a fine craftsman."

"And a good businessman, I hear," Mary said. "So my father says. We heard he just got a contract for building reproduction furniture for some English museum."

"It works out well that Eli and Ruth got *Mam's* share of the shop," Johanna said. "Because she means for Charley and Miriam to take over the farm someday. Charley is a hard worker, and he'll care for the land."

"Both my brothers are good farmers," Mary

said, quickly defending Roland. "They're both hard workers."

"Everyone says Roland has done wonders with that farm," Johanna agreed.

A horse and buggy passed them and turned into the parking lot at the front of the shop. A small boy's face, framed in a straw hat, was pressed against the back window.

Jonah squealed and waved. "*Mam,* it's Benjy! Can I go talk to him?"

"Run on," Johanna said, "but stay out from under the horses' hooves. Don't get dirty, and don't you dare come into service late."

"Me, too," Katy echoed. "I can go, too."

"*Ne.*" Johanna took a firm grip on Katy's hand. "You stay with me."

"There's Lydia." Mary looked to Johanna. "Do you mind if I say hello before service?"

"Of course not. We'll see you inside."

Buggies were lined up on the far side of the parking lot, and women were carrying baskets and covered dishes around the building. Mary called to Lydia Beachy and hurried to help her carry one of the two baskets in her hands. Since it was a fair June day with no sign of rain, they would take the communal after-services meal outside at long tables.

Mam would be coming soon with Susanna, Rebecca and Aunt Jezz. There would be coolers full of ham sandwiches, potato salad, coleslaw, pickled beets and fruit pies. Since no cooking could be done on Church Sunday, all the food for the midday dinner had been prepared the previous day or earlier in the week. *Mam* was bringing a large wedge of cheddar, a three-bean salad, a basket of whoopee pies and—of course—Susanna's anise cookies.

Johanna loved Visiting Sundays, but she also cherished the peace and inner joy of Church Sundays. *Food for the soul.* Singing the old hymns, joining together in prayer with her friends and neighbors, listening to the preachers' sermons—those treasures of the heart gave her the strength to carry on through all the days in between.

Johanna was suddenly filled with thankfulness that she'd been born into the Amish faith and community. *We are a people apart.* People who try to spend each day and each hour serving Him and doing His work on earth in hopes of greater reward in heaven.

"I like church," Katy said, smiling up at her.

"So do I, sweetie," Johanna replied. "So do I."

That day, Uncle Reuben preached on the Good Samaritan, a story from the New Testament that he often chose for his message and one that he could speak on at great length. It was one of Johanna's favorite passages, and she enjoyed his words for the first hour, but as the minutes ticked away and Katy began to wiggle in her lap, Johanna found her attention wandering.

She had chosen a seat near an open window, beside Anna and Mary. Anna's baby, Rose, had fallen asleep, and Johanna couldn't help glancing over at her. Rose was such a precious child, and she brought so much joy to her parents. Johanna loved her dearly—the entire family cherished the little girl—but Johanna couldn't help comparing her to Katy. Next to Rose, Katy seemed so big, no longer a baby, but an adorable little girl. Johanna longed for the baby that Katy had once been, and she longed to cradle another infant—her infant— in her arms.

Uncle Reuben's voice thundered out, echoing off the rafters as he warmed to his subject and began to repeat himself for the third time. Johanna tore her attention from the sleeping babe and tried to focus on her uncle's words. But as her gaze swept the room, she spotted Roland. He wasn't watching Uncle Reuben, either. He was staring directly at her. And when their gazes met, Roland grinned at her.

Startled, Johanna averted her eyes, but when she glanced back from under her lashes, Roland was still watching her. She should have felt disapproval, and she should have let him know that she didn't appreciate his levity during worship, but the truth was, she was secretly pleased. Worse, when Uncle Reuben finally wound up his sermon and the congregation rose to offer the final hymn, she looked at Roland and found him looking at her again, instead of his hymn book.

Anna elbowed her. "Johanna," she whispered as voices raised in praise around them. "Stop flirting and pay attention to service," she admonished. Mischief danced in her eyes. "Stop watching Roland."

"I'm not," Johanna protested, but then she had to stifle a giggle. What was wrong with her? She was acting like a giddy teenager, and it was all Roland Byler's fault.

The hymn ended. Everyone sat down, and Bishop Atlee offered a traditional prayer in High German before dismissing the congregation for the midday break. There would be a short service after the communal meal, but that would consist of prayers, a few more hymns, and everyone would leave by four to head home. As in the morning, the only chores that would be done would be those that were absolutely necessary, mostly involving caring for the children and farm animals.

"*Mam* will have your head," Anna teased as service ended and families rose and gathered their children and belongings.

"She will not. I didn't do anything," Johanna murmured in her sister's ear. "He was staring at me." She reached out for Rose. "Here, let me take her. Your arms must be tired."

Anna passed the sleeping baby, and Johanna cradled her against her chest. Rose never stirred. "She's such a good baby," Anna said. "She slept through Uncle Reuben's entire sermon."

Katy scrambled up on the bench. "Can I hold Rose, *Mam?*" she begged. "Can I?"

"Later, when she's awake," Anna said, stepping around Johanna and sweeping Katy off the bench to safety. "Now I need you to come with me and help me take bread to the tables."

Johanna followed Mary, Anna and Katy. As she passed through the crowded workshop, neighbors stopped her to admire Rose and to exchange news of the past two weeks' doings. There was a crowd of elders at the back of the spacious room, so she turned left to leave by the door that led to the showroom. When she reached the hallway, however, she found Roland alone, arms folded, blocking her way.

"For a woman who isn't interested in me, you spent a lot of time staring at me during service."

Chapter Ten

"I was not staring at you during worship," Johanna said.

"Were, too."

"Was not." She pressed her lips together tightly to stifle a giggle and glanced over her shoulder to be certain no one was too near. She looked back at him. "And I suppose you weren't staring back at me?"

"Me?" Roland smiled that sweet mischievous smile of his, and for a moment, the years fell away and she was looking into the dirty face of the eight-year-old hero who'd chased two bigger English boys at the Delaware State Fair and rescued her *Kapp* from them. "Not me," he teased. "I was watching Preacher Reuben the whole time. I think he preached on the Barren Fig Tree."

"He did not." She could hardly keep from laughing. "Shame on you. You know his sermon was the Good Samaritan."

"Again," they both said together.

Still chuckling, she tried to duck past him, but Roland stretched out both arms and suddenly she was very close to him, with only the still-sleeping Rose between them.

The game was no longer innocent fun. Her heart raced and, for an instant, she thought Roland was going to kiss her. "Please let me go," she whispered. "Someone will see us."

"And what if they do? Why shouldn't we talk to each other? I want to court you, Johanna. I know that if you give yourself the opportunity, you'll fall in love with me all over again."

A whisper of fear raised goose bumps on the nape of her neck. Not fear of Roland, but fear of herself—fear that she wanted him to kiss her. She tightened her grip on Rose. "Don't you think we're too old for courting? I said I was willing to be your wife, but you turned me down. You said you didn't want to marry me." She felt her lower lip tremble and for a moment she feared she'd embarrass herself with tears. "Courting is for couples intending on marrying."

He shook his head. "I didn't say I didn't want to marry you. I never said that. I said I wouldn't marry you for convenience's sake…or because our families think we should marry."

"Roland," she sighed. "I'm not the innocent girl I used to be…the one you want me to be now."

"Excuses. Fears."

The intensity of his gaze made her tremble.

"You're stubborn," he said softly. "You know that we're meant for each other. You're letting that stubbornness stand in the way of real happiness. Happiness for both of us."

A flush of heat shimmered under her skin, and her eyes teared up. *God help me.* And aloud she whispered, "Why can't we just go on being friends?"

Tenderly, Roland brushed a single tear from her cheek. "I can't settle for that. Not with you."

"Why?"

"Because I want you to be my wife…because I want to stand before the bishop…before God… I want us to be a real family, Johanna."

She forced herself to meet his gaze. "I don't know if I even want a husband," she admitted. He was standing so close that she could smell the starch in his shirt. It was a good, clean scent, and it made her even more uncertain…more afraid. If he frightened her now, how much worse would it be if they married?

"Is it taking another husband? Or is it me?"

She tried to think how to answer, but her thoughts were all aflutter. Rose stirred in her arms, and Johanna seized on the excuse. "Let me go," she said. "You'll wake the baby."

"And if I do, you'll soothe her. You were born

to be a mother. I want more children, and I think you do, too. We could have them together, if you'd marry me."

Another baby. The sweet thought of carrying another child in her body—of bringing new life into the world—made her weak. "Don't." Tears clouded her vision as she turned her face away.

"Are you afraid of me?"

"*Ne.* That's *lecherich.* Foolishness. How could I be? It's me…"

"What did your *dat* say?" Roland demanded. "You can't have forgotten. Didn't he tell you to face what frightened you the most? It's what he told me when he taught me to swim."

He moved a step closer, and her breath caught in her throat.

"Let me court you," he said. "If love doesn't grow between us, I'll trouble you no more. But if I'm right, and it's your own stubborn nature keeping us apart, you'll thank me for it."

"Will I?"

Door hinges creaked behind Johanna, and someone cleared her throat. Roland stepped back a decent distance, and Johanna heard her mother say, "There you two are."

"I was just…" Johanna said. *Just what?*

"Roland, they've called you to the first seating for dinner. Bishop Atlee himself asked for you."

Roland nodded. "We'll talk later, Johanna," he said as he strode away.

Her mother eyed her suspiciously. "Is this what I think it is?"

Johanna shook her head. "I didn't meet Roland on purpose, if that's what you're asking. He wants to court me, but I don't know what to do. I'm not sure I want to marry again."

Women's chatter, followed by laughter, drifted through the doorway. *Mam* motioned toward a small room that Eli and Roman used as an office. Johanna followed her in and nudged the door closed behind them. A rainbow of sunlight spilled through a single window and the skylight. Her mother reached for Rose and settled into a rocker, one of the fine spindle-back chairs that Eli designed. Rose slept on.

"You haven't remarried," Johanna said. "You've made a life for yourself without a husband. Why can't I?"

"What is right for me may not be best for you."

"Why not? I've proved I can support myself and my children."

"You're still a young woman. I'm nearly fifty, child. I have eight daughters, counting Grace, an adopted son, four good sons-in-law and a bevy of grandchildren. Your father and I had a strong marriage, a loving marriage. My life is full to overflowing with God's bounty, but you…

you, my precious daughter…you have yet to know that blessing."

"I have a family. Katy and Jonah. You and my sisters and their children. Why do I have to marry again and have a man…" Words failed her.

"Marriage to Wilmer was difficult."

Johanna nodded. Even now, pride kept her from telling her mother just how difficult. What went on between a husband and wife was private, not to be discussed, not even with a mother. "Wilmer called me hardheaded, said that I was an unnatural woman…that I couldn't accept that my husband was God's appointed head of the family."

"Do you believe that you are unnatural?"

"I don't know. Sometimes, maybe." Johanna sat on the floor by her mother's feet and rested her head against her mother's knee. "What if he was right, *Mam?* What if I don't know how to be a proper wife? What if I were to marry Roland and make him as unhappy as I made Wilmer?"

"Roland is a better man than Wilmer ever was. Do you think Roland would ever raise a hand to you in anger?"

"Ne."

"Is he an abuser of alcohol?"

Johanna sighed as her mother's hand rested on her cheek. *"Ne,"* she managed. "Never."

"And you believe him to be a good father—that

he would be a good father to Katy and Jonah as well as his own son?"

"I think… I'm sure he would be." She squeezed her mother's hand, and then got to her feet.

"You loved him once, didn't you?"

Johanna didn't answer…couldn't answer. The truth was too painful to share even with her dear mother.

"All I can tell you is to pray to the Lord for guidance and search your own heart for the answer," *Mam* said. "You're right to be cautious, but know this… With all the love I have from my family, my friends and my church, there are times when I'm lonely. I miss having a partner to care for and to care for me…a man's hand to hold mine when we walk through the orchard after a long day's work. I miss the looks that pass between a husband and wife and the quiet laughter. I'll always love and remember your father. But, I tell you, Johanna, I still have a lot of life left in me. If the right man came along, I would marry again."

Johanna lifted her head and stared at her mother. "You'd take the risk to love again? After *Dat?*"

Her mother laughed. "Life *is* risk, Johanna. Be cautious, follow your conscience, but never stop taking risks. If you do, part of your spirit will wither and die as surely as a garden without rain."

* * *

Monday was so busy that Johanna hardly had time to worry about Roland or the possibility of their marriage. On top of her normal chores—caring for Katy and Jonah, helping Susanna with 'Kota while Grace was at work and school, feeding and looking after her turkeys, bees and sheep—Johanna spent the day helping Ruth. She did her wash and stitched up another two dozen cloth diapers for the expected twins.

On Tuesday morning, she and Rebecca finished a queen-size rose-of-Sharon quilt for an Englisher lady in Salisbury. Then they spent the afternoon making kettles of strawberry-rhubarb jam and mulberry jelly in *Mam's* summer kitchen.

Rebecca, always clever with pen and paint, fashioned hand-printed labels and topped each half-pint jar with a checked cloth cap that fit over the sealed lids. Aunt Jezzy insisted that fancy jars sold for more money and went faster at Spence's than plain ones. If the jams went as well as Aunt Jezzy promised, Johanna decided that she and Rebecca would come up with something equally clever to dress up the honey containers, as well.

Normally, on Tuesdays, Johanna would walk to Roland's to check on the new bee colony, but not this week. The bees at his farm were doing well, and there were plenty of wildflowers and blossoming vegetables and clover to keep them happy.

After Sunday's encounter, she was determined to keep far away from Roland until she made up her mind as to what she wanted to do.

Wednesday, she, Rebecca, Miriam, Susanna and *Mam* scrubbed floors, washed windows, polished woodwork in the entire downstairs of the farmhouse, and washed and ironed all the window curtains. Thursday, she and Katy helped Miriam and Susanna in the garden, planting lima beans, green beans and corn, cutting the last of the spinach, and setting out the eggplant, peppers and late tomatoes that Miriam had started in the greenhouse.

Friday, Johanna packed produce and jam, honey and jellies for Aunt Jezzy's table at the sale and spent the rest of the day cleaning the front and back porch, raking the yard and helping her sisters clean the second floor as thoroughly as they had the first. Since no cooking could be done on Sunday, the Yoder girls worked in the kitchen all day Saturday, baking, churning butter, stirring up a huge kettle of chicken and dumplings, roasting a turkey, and making salads and desserts.

Saturday night, when Johanna knelt beside her bed for her evening prayers, she was tired but pleased at the work she'd managed to do that week. The following day would be a day of rest, a day for laughter and talk, playing quiet games with her children and welcoming friends and relatives.

Sunday began with family prayers around the

kitchen table. It was a beautiful morning, with low humidity and glorious sunshine. Anna and Samuel and the children were coming for supper, and the whole day of fun and visiting stretched before them. As a special treat, Johanna planned to take picnic baskets full of fresh fruit, yogurt, deviled eggs and blueberry muffins to Ruth's house so that they could all share breakfast together—all but Grace and her son. Grace and 'Kota had left early with John to attend the Mennonite church service. Afterward, they were planning to visit John's mother in Pennsylvania, so they wouldn't be back until evening.

Irwin had gone to spend the day with his Beachy cousins, which left *Mam,* Aunt Jezzy, Rebecca, Susanna and the children to go with Johanna to Ruth and Eli's. As they walked down the dirt lane that ran from one house to the other, Johanna was sure that this was God's plan for her. She and her children were happy; they were useful and loved. Surely, risking everything to marry Roland, or anyone else, would be the wrong choice. She'd been truly blessed by the Lord and expecting more of life would be selfish, not to mention foolhardy.

For a few seconds, Johanna felt a wave of sorrow, and the image of Roland's face as she'd seen it last Sunday afternoon formed in her mind. What if he *had* kissed her? What then? What would she have done? But that was past and over. "I have to do what's right for my children," she murmured to Susanna.

"Ya," her little sister agreed with a wide smile.

"This is where I belong," Johanna said, clasping Susanna's chubby hand and squeezing it tight. "Home."

"Ya," Susanna repeated. "Home is *gut.*"

A shiver ran through Johanna. "Home is best," she said. And then, she smiled at Susanna. "I love you, Susanna Banana."

Her sister giggled. "I love you too, Johanna. You are the *bestest* sister."

After such a large breakfast, dinner was light, and everyone was hungry again by suppertime. Eli and Charley had come over to help Irwin set up two long tables end-to-end on *Mam's* lawn. They carried out chairs and benches, and a big rocker for Ruth. She was getting so large with the babies that her back often ached, but she never complained. From her comfortable cushioned chair, Ruth could direct the setting of the table and help with organization.

Johanna had just carried out a large pitcher of lemonade when suddenly Susanna squealed and ran around the corner of the house. A minute later, she was back, walking hand in hand with her friend David.

"King David!" Susanna shouted breathlessly. "King David is here!"

Johanna looked questioningly at her mother. "I didn't know the Kings were coming. We'll have plenty of food, of course, but…"

Hannah shrugged. "I didn't know, either." She rose to welcome David and his parents, but the only other person to round the house was Jonah, kicking his soccer ball.

Susanna tugged David across the lawn to where Hannah stood. "King David," she repeated. Susanna was smiling so hard that Johanna was afraid her face would crack. "My friend."

"It's good to see you, David," Johanna said. "Are your father and mother coming?"

"I *in-vited* him," Susanna said with emphasis. "I did. I said, come to visit."

"*Ne.* Not my *mam.* Not my *dat.* Just…just me." David grinned at Susanna. "Come to visit Sunday. Her." David wore his go-to-church black trousers, high-top black leather shoes, white shirt and black vest. Under his straw hat, Johanna could see the gold rim of his paper crown. David was so excited that his speech, never as clear as Susanna's, was difficult to understand, but it seemed that Susanna understood every word he said.

"King David and me," Susanna proclaimed. "We're walking. Us. Walking out."

"We can talk about that later," Hannah said

gently, stepping between Susanna and David. "I think David is thirsty. You should get him something cold to drink."

"Want birch beer?" Susanna asked. "*Mam* makes good birch beer." She giggled, wrinkled her nose and shook her head. "Not beer beer. Soda-pop beer." When David nodded vigorously, they went in search of the soda.

Soon Miriam arrived with Anna and *Grossmama* and the children. Mae and Lori Ann had brought the rag dolls that Anna had sewn for them, complete with changes of clothing, white *Kapps* and small black bonnets. Katy was ecstatic when *Grossmama* pulled an identical doll out of her bag and presented it to her.

"I made the *Kapps*," Naomi said shyly. "*Grossmama* showed me how."

Soon, the three little girls had carried their dolls to the grape arbor to play house and *Grossmama* was seated under the tree near Ruth. Jonah was happily trailing after Samuel's twin sons, who were setting up a croquet game on the grass between the tables and the garden. Rebecca had found a copy of *Black Beauty* for Naomi, and she was happily reading on the back step, while Johanna and Ruth took turns holding baby Rose.

The boys had their game set up and were just starting to teach Jonah how to hit the wooden ball through the hoops when another visitor arrived. It was Nip Hilty, of all people.

"Who is that?" *Grossmama* called loudly. "I don't know him."

Aunt Jezzy leaped to her feet, fluttered her hands, and turned as red as a jar of pickled beets. She was so flustered that she just stood there, seemingly unable to greet her guest. *Mam* stepped into the breach, smiling and walking to meet him. "It's good to have you visit, Nip," she said.

Johanna glanced at Rebecca. Her sister shrugged, and behind them, Miriam twittered.

"Who do you think invited him?" Miriam whispered.

"She knows about Nip and Aunt Jezzy," Rebecca murmured to Johanna. "I'm telling you, it's scary. Nothing gets by *Mam*."

"I don't know you," *Grossmama* repeated from her chair. "Are you from Pennsylvania?" It was her standard question when she met someone she didn't recognize. "Do you know my son Jonas? He's milking the cows, but he'll be up in time for supper."

Nip was all smiles as he approached the other women. "You may not know me, but I know you. My late wife had a cousin in Ohio who's friends with your sister Ida. She said Lovina Yoder was the finest braid-rug maker she'd ever known and it was a crying shame that she moved to Delaware."

Grossmama blinked. "Ida. Your wife knows Ida?" *Grossmama's* eyes narrowed and she peered at Nip over her wire-frame glasses. "Ida makes rugs, but hers don't hold a candle to mine. I teach the Englishers at the Senior Center. I live with my son Jonah. That's his wife." She pointed at Ruth. "And this is my grandchild." She indicated Rose, now sleeping in Ruth's arms. "I'm going to show her how to braid rugs."

Nip sighed and hooked a thumb through his left suspender. "My wife would have been pleased to come to your classes, Lovina, but she died."

Grossmama was still taking him in. "Was she a faithful daughter to the church?"

"She was," Nip answered.

"Then she's in a better place." *Grossmama* seemed to then notice Aunt Jezzy's distress. "That's my sister," *Grossmama* pointed out. "But not Ida."

"Jezzy," Nip supplied. He glanced at Aunt Jezzy and smiled.

"Folks think she's odd," *Grossmama* continued in Pennsylvania *Deutch.* "Never married."

"I can't think why," Nip said, "as fine a woman as she is."

Grossmama tapped her forehead and whispered loudly. "*Narrisch.* Crazy."

"*Ne.*" Nip threw another admiring glance at the

still-silent Aunt Jezzy. "*So schlau wie ein fuchs—*smart like a fox."

"I have to agree," came a man's voice from behind Johanna. She turned to see Roland standing there with J.J. on his shoulders.

"Roland?" Johanna said. "I didn't expect you today."

Roland grinned as he lowered his son to the grass. "Well, I'm here," he said. "Here and starving for some Yoder good cooking." He cut his eyes at Hannah, a sly smirk on his face now. "I guess she must have forgotten to mention that she invited us."

Chapter Eleven

Johanna threw her mother a questioning look, and a lump of emotion rose in Roland's throat. He was struck by how beautiful Johanna was, with her curling auburn hair tucked modestly beneath her *Kapp,* her apron crisp and white against the soft blue of her calf-length dress, and the dusting of golden freckles over her nose and cheeks.

"I invited J.J. and Roland," Hannah said, answering Johanna's unspoken question and flashing him a genuine smile. "It's been too long since they broke bread at our table."

Roland grinned. "She knew we'd be eating cheese-and-bologna sandwiches again tonight and took pity on us." Seeing Hannah, still so lively and rosy-cheeked in her middle age, made it easy to see why her daughters were all so attractive. *When Johanna is Hannah's age,* he thought, *she'll still be the loveliest* hausfrau *in the county.* But whether she would be his *frau* or not was yet to be seen.

"It's good to have you, Roland," Hannah continued. "Samuel tells me that you've been offered a contract with Windward Farms."

Johanna's eyes widened with interest. "A contract?" she asked. "I hadn't heard."

"Ya." Roland tried not to sound as though he was boasting. "You know Windward Farms? The big horse farm with the white fences on Fox Meadow Road? Their farrier is retiring, and John Hartman recommended me to take his place. I've been up there a couple of times, and I guess they liked my work."

"No reason why they shouldn't. Everyone says you're the best farrier in the county." Johanna smiled warmly at J.J. "Jonah and the big boys are playing croquet. I'm sure they'd like you to join them." And then to Roland, "I was just going inside to get the ice cream churn. We promised the children strawberry ice cream for dessert. Would you mind carrying it out for me?"

"Of course not." He lowered his son to the ground. "Go on," he said to J.J. "But stay out of mischief, and don't make a pest of yourself."

"I'm going that way. I'll go with you."

Hannah held out her hand and Roland watched them walk away. Raising a child on his own wasn't easy, and J.J. had been through more than most boys his age. His mother had always babied him, and losing her was a terrible blow. Now, acting as both mother and father, Roland never knew whether he was being too hard on the boy or too easy.

The elders quoted verses from the Bible that instructed a father not to spare the rod, but he was too soft to take a switch to J.J.'s tender skin. Johanna was a loving mother, and her children were well behaved, but spirited. If what he hoped for came to pass, and she did agree to become his wife, he was sure she'd be good for his son.

"Roland? The ice cream churn?"

Johanna had started back toward the house and he quickened his step to catch up. "I would have told you that we were coming, but I didn't see you after Hannah asked us." Johanna pushed open the gate and moved through it ahead of him, and his gaze fastened on the tiny russet curls at the nape of her neck. "Are you unhappy that we're here?" he asked, afraid of what she would say.

"Ne."

Relief seeped through him. "Are you glad?"

She ascended the back steps to the porch and then opened the screen door. Only then did she glance back at him over her shoulder. "You ask the strangest questions for a man," she observed. "Why wouldn't I be happy to have an old friend and his son visit us?"

He shook his head. "You aren't an easy woman to court, Johanna Yoder."

"Detweiler," she softly corrected. A wrinkle crinkled the smooth skin between her brows. "You forget Wilmer."

"I'd like to forget him," he agreed, standing at the bottom of the steps, looking up at her. "I wish he'd never come to Seven Poplars and that you'd never married him."

She gave a graceful shrug. "But then I wouldn't have Katy or Jonah. And they are the dearest things in this world to me."

"As they should be. I didn't mean it that way. They are wonderful children. Being a mother is part of who you are, but you'll always be one of the Yoder girls to me—the finest one."

A peach blush spread over her cheeks, but Roland could tell by the gleam in her eyes that she was pleased. Johanna hesitated, half in and half out of the doorway, her slim hands gripping the wooden frame of the screen door. She averted her gaze and then looked up at him from under thick lashes. "You shouldn't say such things."

"But lying is a sin." He placed a hand protectively over one of hers.

"And so is pride." She slid the captured hand out from under his, leaving him with the memory of her touch. "You'll tempt me to have foolish thoughts," she said.

"If there's a sin for saying what I believe, I'll pay the price."

She shook her head and tried to assume a disapproving expression, but he knew her too well. Johanna could never hide her feelings from him. "You always had the knack for saying the right things to all the girls," she said, as the corners of her mouth tugged upward into the hint of a smile. "Even to the ones who were…plain. And that was something I liked about you."

"Not you, Johanna. You were never plain."

She moved into the kitchen and again, he followed. It was warm in there. Not a breeze stirred the curtains through the open windows, but Roland could feel the buzz of tension between them, and he had the urge to kiss her. He remembered the sweet taste of her lips and the way she'd felt in his arms. An aching rose inside him. He wanted her to be his wife, and if he couldn't have her, he didn't know how he could face the rest of his life.

She turned to face him and recognition flickered in Johanna's eyes. He knew with certainty that she felt the same thrumming in the still air that he did. Her lips parted, and she uttered a small sigh as she took a step backward. "There," she said brusquely as she pointed to the wooden churn standing on the counter. "It's heavy. We've already packed the ice and salt around the barrel."

Roland took a moment to collect himself and

then lifted the churn off the counter. "It's not that heavy," he said. Beads of condensation gathered on the outside of the wooden container, soaking through his thin shirt and cooling his skin. "Is this the same one your *dat* used to make ice cream when we were kids?" He gazed intensely into Johanna's eyes. "I remember the afternoon he made blueberry ice cream and Charley and I went home with blue lips and tongues."

"Ya." She chuckled. "The same one. A wheelwright built them in Lancaster back in the twenties. He did good work. The metal crank still turns as easily as it ever did."

"That was a *gut* day, when we had the blueberry ice cream. I remember that Jonas built a fire when it got dark and let us make popcorn and toast marshmallows on willow sticks."

"And we chased lightning bugs and put them in glass jars so they blinked on and off in the dark like lanterns. Remember? *Dat* made us let them all go before bedtime. He was so kind he didn't want to see even a lightning bug hurt needlessly." Johanna's face softened, and the years fell away so that he could see the laughing girl she'd been that night—teasing and merry, without a care in the world.

"We could do that again tonight," he said. "Catch lightning bugs. The children would like it. It seems as though there are a lot of them this summer. And early in the season to see so many."

"Children or lightning bugs?" she teased.

Roland grip tightened on the churn. He shivered as the cold seeped through to his chest. "Johanna…" His voice grew husky. "I want to—"

"Mam!" Katy's small voice came through the screen door. *"Mam,* are you in here?"

"Ya," Johanna answered. Her gaze shifted from the entrance back to meet his. "Here, Katy."

Roland saw the tautness go out of Johanna's shoulders, and he knew that she welcomed her daughter's interruption.

"We're coming," Johanna said with forced cheerfulness.

Roland fought a momentary feeling of disappointment. For a second there, things had been right between them…as easy and comfortable as it used to be. And, foolishly, he'd hoped…

She crossed the kitchen and opened the door. "Roland's going to make ice cream for us." He couldn't see the little girl, but he heard her excited giggles. "And tonight, when it gets dark, we're all going to catch lightning bugs. Would you like that?"

Johanna stepped back, pulling the door open even wider so that he could pass through. As he did, she smiled up at him. "Strawberry ice cream, this time. Will it taste as good as blueberry, do you think?"

His heartbeat quickened at the warm affection in her eyes, and hope flared in his chest. He scrambled to think of something to say that wouldn't take away from the moment. "At least it won't turn our lips blue," he managed, and was rewarded by the sound of her soft chuckle.

Whatever that feeling of warmth had been that had passed between Roland and Johanna in the kitchen changed everything. He had followed her into the house, afraid he didn't belong there, no matter how much he wanted to be. But when they rejoined the family, he slipped into his old place of years ago among the Yoders, just as easily as shaping a horseshoe at his own forge.

Susanna and her friend David were sitting at the end of the table, their heads close together, giggling and playing with a cat's cradle, a loop of yarn that first one and then the other would try to twist into different patterns. David's straw hat lay on the bench beside him, and his familiar paper crown hung precariously over one ear, but no one seemed to notice. Ruth, Hannah and Rebecca were admiring Anna's baby girl, cuddled in her mother's lap at the other end of the table, and J.J., face earnest, was trying desperately to drive a yellow ball through a series of hoops on the lawn while Jonah and Samuel's twins shouted advice.

Roland noted, to his surprise, that Nip Hilty and Johanna's Aunt Jezzy were seated together in the old porch swing that someone had carried out to the backyard. Nip was whittling a length of wood and talking a blue streak while she listened intently. He didn't know what they found so mutually interesting, but it was clear to him that both of them were enjoying the interlude. Johanna's grandmother was seated near them in a lawn chair, but she'd fallen asleep, her chin on her chest, snoring softly.

Charley, Samuel, Miriam and Eli were talking near the grape arbor. Roland heard snatches of their conversation. A discussion had arisen in the church as to whether a tractor with iron wheels could be used to power farm equipment, as some of the other Old Order Amish groups allowed. From what Roland could gather, Charley and Miriam favored the change, but Samuel didn't.

Later in the month, Roland knew he'd be called upon to vote on the question. Although women could be full members of the church, they weren't allowed to have a say in such matters, so Miriam's opinion didn't count, other than her influence on Charley or the male members of her family. Which was probably why she was the one talking the most. Roland hadn't made up his mind yet, but—in any case—the final decision would come from Bishop Atlee. The vote was only meant to help him make his decision. Whatever he decided would be part of the *Ordnung,* and the entire community would obey.

"Will this do?" Johanna asked, drawing Roland's attention back to the task at hand. She pointed to a small picnic table, one usually used for the children.

"Perfect," Roland answered. If she'd asked, he would have churned the ice cream while standing in the duck pond or balancing on top of the chicken house. What mattered was that he and Johanna were doing something together, something fun, without arguing.

She cleared the plates and glasses to one side and he placed the churn on the table and began to turn the crank. It usually took between twenty and thirty minutes to turn the milk, cream, sugar and strawberries into ice cream, and the cranking grew more difficult as the mixture hardened. Fortunately, the years of swinging a hammer in his craft as a farrier had given him strong arms. One of Samuel's twins brought a bucket of cracked ice and a box of salt, so they could stop and refill the outer chamber as the ice melted.

With Johanna there, the time went by all too fast. When the ice cream was ready, they packed the churn into a washtub, added the remaining ice and swaddled the whole thing in an old blanket. Then they stowed it in the shade under the grape arbor to freeze solid, and everyone gathered around the table for supper.

Hannah waved Roland to a place on the bench beside J.J. and Jonah, directly across the table from Johanna and Katy. The only thing better would have been to be seated beside Johanna. But that was rarely done in their community because the women had to get up and down to bring food from the kitchen or serve the guests and family.

Roland ate until he thought he would burst, and then he had two slices of Johanna's peach-and-rhubarb pie with strawberry ice cream on top. The children pronounced the ice cream the best they'd ever eaten, and Roland felt pleased that he'd been able to add something to the wonderful Sunday supper.

Afterward, the adults rested on blankets spread on the grass and the children played around them. The sun was already behind the trees, and twilight filled the Yoder farm with a delightful peacefulness. Susanna and David joined the youngsters at a final game of croquet before it got too dark to see the wire hoops, and the little girls crept under the table to play house with their dolls.

"I think I'll check on my bees," Johanna said to Roland. "Would you like to walk back to the hives with me?"

"I'd like that." He glanced at Hannah to see if she would object, but she was engaged in conversation with Anna and Ruth. Aunt Jezzy and Nip had claimed their seat on the swing again and, once more, Nip was talking and whittling while she provided a willing audience.

Johanna bent and peered under the table. "Katy, we're taking a walk. Do you want to come with us?"

"Ne, Mam," Roland heard a small voice reply. "Want to play babies with Mae and Lori Ann."

"All right." Johanna dropped the tablecloth. "If you need anything, go to Aunt Rebecca."

"Mam!" Jonah called. "When are we going to catch lightning bugs?"

"Soon," Johanna promised. "We have to wait until it gets dark enough so that you can see them." She smiled at Roland as they walked away from the others and around the house. "It was a good idea," she said. "The kids are so excited. I can't believe we haven't thought to do it yet this summer."

"You're a busy woman," he said. "What with your bees, turkeys and sheep and quilts, I don't know anyone who works any harder."

Johanna shrugged. "Anna. I don't know where she gets her energy, and her with five older children *and* a new baby."

"She has Naomi to help her, and Rebecca. And

I heard Samuel say one of his cousins was sending a daughter out to give Anna a hand in the house."

"Esther Mast. *Ya,* she is," Johanna agreed. "She's seventeen or eighteen. She was here visiting last summer, and she and Anna got on well. She's strong and willing and good with the children. *Mam's* offered to let her stay with us since Grace will be leaving us soon. That way Esther can have her own room."

"Not many young women would want to leave home to do chores at someone else's house. She must be good-natured."

"She comes from a big family and they live in a small community in Missouri. I think there are six or seven girls. Her mother thinks Anna's the perfect person to teach her how to run a house, and I think Esther wants to see a new part of the country before she settles down and gets married."

They crossed the barnyard and started down the lane that led to the orchard. Roland heard the bleat of a lamb in the sheepfold and the answering call of its mother. Overhead, wings fluttered as pigeons returned to their roosts in the attic of the granary. The smells were familiar and sweet, the scent of new-cut hay, horses and honeysuckle. For the first time in a long while, Roland felt content.

He glanced at Johanna, and when she smiled back at him, he reached out and took her hand. To his surprise, she didn't pull away or protest.

They walked on without speaking, enjoying the quiet of the fading day, and Roland laced his fingers around hers and savored the warm feel of her hand in his.

When they reached the first of her beehives, long shadows of evening has already fallen over the white wooden boxes, and the bees were quiet except for a low, contented buzzing. She remained next to him, still very close, and Roland looked down at her. "They don't seem to be awake," he said.

"I didn't think they would be."

"Then why—"

Her chuckle was soft and light, and he found himself chuckling with her. "You've been dragged out here under false pretenses," she said.

"Does this mean we're courting?" he asked. His breath caught in his throat as he waited for her answer.

"Ne," she murmured. "I'm not ready for that yet, but I wanted to see what it would feel like— to have you hold my hand. It's been so long."

"Since Wilmer?"

She shook her head. He could no longer see the expression in her eyes because it was too dark, but he felt the sadness radiating from her. "I wasn't thinking of Wilmer," she admitted. "I was thinking of you and me. Wilmer wasn't that kind of man…he wasn't one to make a show of affection."

Roland was struck by the foolishness of the man, and for a few seconds he allowed himself to pity Wilmer. "Not even with his wife?"

She sighed. "We need more time like this," she said, leaving his question unanswered. "You and I."

He threaded his fingers through hers. "And what would you have done if I hadn't tried to hold your hand?"

"I suppose I would have had to make the first move." And then, before he could think of something clever to say, she went on. "Jonah and Katy would love to go to the ocean. Do you think we might hire a driver and take them to the beach next weekend?"

"You want us to go together?"

She chuckled. "With the children. And J.J., of course. I thought to ask Aunt Jezzy to come along with us."

"I'm nearly thirty, both of us were married before and with children. Do we still need a chaperone?"

Her chuckle became a merry laugh. "Susanna would probably like to go with us, as well. But if you'd rather not—"

"We'll go," he said quickly. "Of course we'll go. And there's no need to wait until next Saturday. I don't have any farrier work to do Wednesday. Could we go Wednesday? All of us?"

"Susanna, too?"

"And your mother, if you like. I want to be with you, Johanna. Whatever it takes to get you to trust me again, I'll do."

"I think it would be good for us," she said. "It would be fun." She let go of his hand and turned back toward the house. "And now we have lightning bugs and children to chase."

"Johanna, wait." He caught hold of her and pulled her into his arms. He felt her tremble in his arms as he lowered his mouth toward hers.

"Are you kissing?" Susanna's voice came out of the darkness. "No kissing, Johanna." She appeared out of the darkness, followed by a bulky shadow that could only be David. "*Mam* said, 'No kissing!' And if I can't kiss David, you can't kiss Roland."

And then they all laughed.

Chapter Twelve

"Towels. Don't forget towels. And make Jonah wear his hat on the beach," Hannah advised. "I put a bottle of sunscreen in your bag. I hope it will be enough for everyone."

"We'll be fine, *Mam*," Johanna assured her. "I promise they won't come back the color of cranberries."

Hannah paused in the center of the kitchen, laundry basket in hand, and smiled at her. "I know they will both love the ocean," she said. "And you have such a pretty day for an outing." She looked as though she wanted to say something else, but was biting her tongue.

"What is it, *Mam*?" Johanna chuckled. "Out with it, before you burst."

"You have a good time, too. You and Roland. You deserve it."

Johanna pushed the canning jar full of ice deep

into the cooler that was resting on the kitchen table. "We're not walking out if that's what you mean. Don't start counting celery stalks yet."

"So you're still unsure?" Hannah lowered the wicker basket to the floor. "Sunday night, when the two of you were chasing lightning bugs on the lawn…when you tripped over that croquet hoop and Roland caught you…it seemed like—"

"Like I was having a good time," Johanna finished for her mother. "I was. It was a wonderful evening. Like old times."

"Ne," Hannah said gently. "Not like old times. Neither of you are children anymore. You're a grown woman with two children, and Roland is a father and a widower. Maybe…new times?"

Johanna squeezed a quart of canned peaches into the corner of the cooler. Roland had insisted on paying for the van and driver, so she had insisted on packing lunch for them all. The only difficult part was choosing foods that would stay cool enough in the summer heat not to spoil. She kept her menu simple: hard-boiled eggs, bread, cheese, fruit, carrot strips and whoopie pies with marshmallow filling that she and Susanna had made the previous night. She was taking plenty to drink, too—a gallon of lemonade and another of fresh well water.

"Johanna?"

She sighed and looked up to meet her mother's

shrewd gaze. "I think I still care for Roland," she admitted, and then corrected herself. "I know I do. But I'm afraid." She opened her arms and let them fall to her sides. "I'm afraid of making the wrong decision again and..."

"Afraid Roland will disappoint you as Wilmer did?"

"Ne." Johanna shook her head. "He's nothing like Wilmer. I know Roland would never hurt me physically, and he isn't sick in the head like poor Wilmer was. But it's hard to forget what my bad choice brought upon me and how much it hurt me. It's hard to consider placing myself and my children in another man's hands. Even Roland's."

"Yet, our teachings bid us that the husband and father must be the head of the family, and a good wife must listen to her husband's wishes."

She pushed aside the containers to make room for the sealed plastic container of whoopie pies, closed the cooler lid and latched it. "I know that, *Mam,*" she said. "But what if I can't be a good wife? What if it's better for all of us if I leave things as they are?" She didn't want to talk about this today, and especially not with *Mam.* It was too difficult. Just thinking about Roland was too difficult. Today was supposed to be fun, a day when she didn't have to be serious or make decisions that would change the rest of her life.

Hannah came close and hugged her. "You must

follow your heart, my dear, dear child. And your head. But if you keep Roland waiting too long, he'll choose another—perhaps even that girl from Lancaster that Rebecca and Aunt Jezzy say is always talking to him at Spence's. Roland is a young man with responsibilities. He must take a wife and he must do it soon."

"If he wants to marry that silly Lancaster girl, let him do it and be done with it. I refuse to be pushed into a hasty decision that I might live to regret."

Hannah hugged her even tighter and whispered, "Do as you will, Johanna. You always have. No matter what, I'll always love you, and I'll always be here for you. But if this goes badly, just don't say that I didn't warn you." With a final squeeze, her mother let her go.

As you did about Wilmer? Johanna gritted her teeth and swallowed the sharp answer that rose in her throat. *Mam* wasn't one to say *I told you so.* She knew her mother had been right. She'd known it then and she knew it now. She'd married Wilmer—a man she hardly knew—to salve the ache breaking up with Roland had caused her. *Mam* had warned her that Wilmer was too rigid.

"I'm sorry," Hannah murmured. "I'm an interfering woman. The Lord knows it's a fault I've struggled with all my life. I love my children, and I think I know best how they should solve their problems." She forced a chuckle. "The truth is that I don't, Johanna. I was wrong to speak so. You're old enough to know your own mind."

Johanna smiled back at her. "I should be," she said. "But it was a lot easier when I was a girl, and all I had to do was listen to you and *Dat* and do as I was told."

Hannah rolled her eyes. "As if that was ever so." Her laughter became genuine. "Oh, my sweet girl. You, I'm afraid, are too much like me. Too stubborn and willful for our own good. As my father always said, 'You, Hannah, are a trial to your parents, but a greater one to yourself. You'd cut off your own nose to spite your face.'"

The children were so excited when they tumbled out of the van at Delaware Seashore State Park that they were bouncing up and down like jumping jacks. "You look after the kids," Roland said, "and I'll get the coolers and the canopy."

Susanna and Aunt Jezzy ushered Jonah, Katy and J.J. out of the parking lot and onto the beach. Johanna handed each of them a towel and retied Katy's bonnet, which was in danger of blowing off. There was a brisk breeze off the ocean, and Johanna doubted that the boys' straw hats would stay on for long. Being bareheaded could be a real problem for Jonah with his fair skin. Both Katy and J.J. were better off, having a complexion that tanned rather than burned. Luckily, she had the sunscreen her mother had packed and she quickly applied it to their faces, arms and legs.

"Look, *Mam!*" Jonah pointed toward the inlet. "That man caught a fish!"

"And there's a big boat," J.J. chimed in. "I wish we could go on it."

Roland and the driver, Mike, unloaded the bag containing the canopy and carried it across the sand to a place about fifty feet from the water's edge. Johanna instructed the children to remove their shoes and stockings and then took them all down to play in the waves, while the two men set up the canopy and went back to the van for the coolers.

Roland had suggested they spend the day at the state park at Indian River rather than Rehoboth Beach because there would be fewer Englishers to stare and point at the quaint Amish. Johanna was glad that he had. The beach was nearly deserted: a young man was searching the dune area with a metal detector, and the couple sleeping on a blanket near the high-tide mark didn't even look up at the children's shouts of joy.

"Don't go out too far," Johanna warned.

Susanna echoed, "Too far!"

Soon, Johanna, Susanna and Aunt Jezzy joined the two boys in a game of Catch Me if You Can with the incoming waves, and Katy simply sat down on the damp sand and let the foamy salt water wash over her. Jonah and J.J. quickly became wet to their waists, and, as Johanna had feared, their hats flew off in the wind. Laughing, Susanna ran to chase them down, as Roland and the driver brought the last cooler down to the shade of the canopy.

"What did you pack in here?" Roland asked. "Rocks?"

"Food, silly," Susanna shouted back as she captured J.J.'s hat. Then, she squealed and pointed toward the parking lot.

A second van pulled up beside Mike's and the horn honked. The doors opened and more family poured out. Johanna recognized a waving Charley, Miriam and the identical red mops of Samuel's twins. 'Kota skipped along beside Miriam, but who was the other Amish man, seated in the front seat? It couldn't be Eli or Samuel. He wasn't tall enough.

Taking hold of Katy's hand and calling to J.J. and Jonah, Johanna walked back up the beach to meet the others. To her surprise, the man turned out to be Nip Hilty. Johanna turned back to see Aunt Jezzy splashing in the waves as she spun around three times and then reached down to grab handfuls of foam and toss them in the air. "Aunt Jezzy, look who it is," she called.

"I know." Her aunt giggled. "Nip said he was

going to get a driver." And then, she turned away and began to walk down the beach picking up shells.

"Look! Look!" Susanna shrieked as one more person got out of the van. "It's my King David. He came! He came!"

"Not more food!" Roland exclaimed as they watched Charley and Rudy unload another cooler from their vehicle. "We'll never eat it all. We'll have to stay a week."

"We hope you don't mind," Miriam said as she came toward Johanna. "Nip invited us. It seemed like such a good idea, that Charley took the day off, and we sort of picked up a few more nephews on the way." Miriam reached into her bag and produced a blue pail full of plastic sand molds and a shovel. "This is for you, little Katy-did," she said, handing them to her. "You're the only little girl here today so I think you deserve a special treat for putting up with all these boys."

"You know we're glad to have you." Johanna glanced down at Katy. "What do you say to Aunt Miriam for bringing you a present?"

"I'm not little. I'm big." She glanced up at her mother and realized her error. *"Danke,"* she said quickly.

"I've got a bucket, too," 'Kota declared. "Want to make a sand castle, Katy?"

"Don't you want to go in the water with the boys?" Johanna asked him.

'Kota shook his head. "Nope. Want to build a castle."

"Me, too," Katy agreed. "Build a...a...house!"

It seemed like chaos, but soon, the coolers were opened, cold lemonade and apples were handed around, and Susanna, David and the children all ran back to the water, supervised by Miriam, Charley, Aunt Jezzy and Nip. Katy and 'Kota settled down to construct a farmyard and duck pond in the wet sand.

"If you dig a ditch and then a hole for your pond," Roland explained, "the waves will come in and fill it for you." He crouched down beside 'Kota and showed him where to begin his trench.

Katy dug furiously, piling sand to make her house, while Johanna brought buckets of seawater to wet the sand and make it easier to mold. It wasn't long before she and Roland were as wet as the children, much to the kids' delight. Roland rolled his pants to his knees, but then a big wave broke and splashed the entire front of his shirt and sent water rolling down his beard.

J.J. and Jonah soon joined the fun, expanding the canal to reach more hastily dug ponds. Soon, Nip discovered a small piece of driftwood and with his penknife quickly whittled a tiny boat, which he presented to Aunt Jezzy. She set it adrift in 'Kota's duck pond, to his and Katy's delight. After that, nothing would do but that he made boats for Jonah and J.J. as well, and there was a frantic search for more bits of suitable whittling material.

Jonah, expanding his canal, came upon a strange creature buried in the sand and called Johanna to see it. "What is it, *Mam?* Will it bite?"

She laughed. "It's a sand flea."

Katy wrinkled her nose. "Not a flea, *Mam.* Too big."

"It's little. Be gentle," Johanna cautioned. It began to wiggle and Jonah dropped it, and then shrieked with glee as it scurried away on spindly legs and began to tunnel down into the sand at the waterline.

The wind died down enough for the boys to put their hats back on, and Roland showed them how to look for bubbles in the wet sand and dig for clams. They didn't find any clams, but they did see a small fish, which swam back out to sea on the next wave. The boys howled in disappointment, but Katy laughed and clapped, shouting, "Swim away, fish. Swim away."

"When do we eat?" Charley asked. "I'm starving."

"You're always starving," Miriam teased.

"Me, too," David said. "Me!"

"All right," Johanna agreed. "Let's go have our lunch."

Everyone trooped back to the canopy and dove into the contents of the two coolers. Roland and Nip poured cups of cold water all around and after a brief moment of silent prayer, they began to make short work of every bite that Miriam and Johanna had packed. Afterward, the women took the children up to the bathrooms, washed their hands and faces, and returned to join the others.

The children were all for returning to the ocean at once, but the adults were adamant. No one could go back into the water until they'd rested for at least half an hour. Nip produced a pocket watch and became the official timekeeper. Katy curled up in Johanna's lap and fell asleep, one small hand still tightly clasping the handle of her blue shovel.

At last the thirty minutes was up, and the kids, all but a sleepy Katy, ran back toward the water, eager to get as wet and sandy as possible. Johanna got to her feet and was about to follow them, when Roland gestured to her. "Come walk with me," he said.

Johanna hesitated. She did want to walk on the beach, but she was responsible for her children. She glanced at Miriam. "Is it all right if…"

Miriam smiled. "Go on. Take some time for

yourself. We'll watch the kids. Go. Have fun. You always loved the ocean. Enjoy it."

"Jonah doesn't always do what—"

Charley laughed. "It's fine, Johanna. Go with Roland. I think between us, we can handle a few small kids."

"If we don't get some practice, how will we know what to do with our own when God sends them?" Miriam asked.

Miriam could have passed for sixteen today. She hadn't worn a bonnet, but had braided her hair, pinned it up and covered it with a scarf. Somehow, she'd managed to lose the pins on one side, and that braid had tumbled down. Undaunted, Miriam had removed the bobby pins on the other side so that both braids hung down over her shoulders. She looked happy, Johanna thought, very happy. Who would have believed that Miriam would be so satisfied in her marriage to Charley, a boy she'd known all her life…a boy she'd told everyone was her best friend?

Why her and not me? Johanna wondered. How was Miriam so wise in picking a husband? Johanna had been certain that Miriam was going to choose John Hartman. If anyone was reckless enough to marry out of the church and leave the faith, she would have expected it to be Miriam, not Leah. *It's like* Grossmama *always says,* she mused. *Only God knows what's in another person's heart.*

"Johanna?" Roland held out a hand.

"Coming." She followed him, but didn't take his hand. He strode off in the direction of the inlet, and she matched him step for step, the wind tearing at her bonnet until she untied it and wrapped the ribbons around her fingers. Removing the heavy bonnet was a relief. She stopped, closed her eyes and inhaled deeply, savoring the taste of salt in the air. "I love the ocean," she said, opening her eyes again and looking up at Roland.

"I love you," he said. Or...she thought he said it.

Johanna felt her cheeks grow warm, despite the cool breeze. "You shouldn't say such things," she admonished. "It's not decent."

"What things?" He arched a brow mischievously. "What did I say?"

"That...that you..." She broke off and looked away. What if she were wrong? What if she'd imagined it? She'd already asked him to marry her. What if he hadn't said that at all and she called him on it? What kind of fast woman would she look like to suggest he'd...

"I'm teasing you, Johanna." His face crinkled in a grin. "Are you having a good time today?" He began walking again and she did the same.

Safer ground. "Ya," she answered. "A wonderful time. The best day ever. The children—"

"Not the children. *You.* Are *you* enjoying yourself?" he demanded.

"I am." She smiled back at him. "Thank you."

The sound of the tide rushing through the inlet grew louder the closer they got, and the air felt cooler. Roland reached out and took her hand, and this time she didn't protest. They reached the edge of the rocks, and he climbed up and helped her to a ledge where they had a better view of the dark, surging water. The giant boulder felt warm and solid beneath her, and she sat and curled her legs up under her skirt. Her dress was wrinkled but nearly dry.

They sat there, not speaking, her hand in his, with the sun on their faces and the powerful crash and curl of the inlet washing around them. It was Roland who finally broke the comfortable silence. "Well, Johanna Yoder. I'd say our courting is going pretty well, wouldn't you?"

She threw him a look. "Who says we're courting?"

"I do."

"And you're the judge of that?"

"I know you better than you think."

She sniffed. "You, Roland Byler, are entirely too fond of your own ideas."

"No argument. All I said was the truth. We're courting. Everyone knows it. Even your mother

knows it. You're just too stubborn to admit when I'm right."

"You're saying I'm stubborn?"

He said nothing; he just looked at her.

She chuckled. "I suppose I am." Her eyes narrowed. "But courting doesn't mean marriage. I haven't made up my mind yet, and until I do—"

"It's because of what happened before, isn't it? Because of what I did in Pennsylvania when I almost got arrested? How many times do I have to tell you that I didn't intend to—"

"Ne." She pulled her hand out of his. "I don't want to talk about it. Not today. Don't spoil it for me. Please don't."

"I just want you to understand that I—"

She put a finger to her lips. "Shh. Not another word about what happened in Lancaster or you can sit on this rock by yourself."

"If you feel that way." His shoulders stiffened.

"I do. I came to have fun, not to remember bad times." She offered him a half smile. "We couldn't have done anything today that would have made me happier."

He nodded. "I'm glad."

His features remained strained and she knew that she'd hurt him. She hadn't wanted to…at least she hoped she hadn't. This time, she was the one who reached out a hand. "I do love you, Roland."

"Then you'll be my wife?"

She looked at their hands clasped together. "I don't know. I'm still trying to decide."

"How long? When will you know?"

She leaned forward and brushed her lips against his. "I can't say, Roland, but when I do decide, you'll be the first one I tell."

Chapter Thirteen

On Friday, Johanna sat on the grass by Roland's pond, with J.J. beside her. It was midmorning, and the day promised to be another hot one, with no sign of rain, which the crops and gardens could all use. The sun was shining, and white, lacy clouds drifted lazily across a robin's-egg-blue sky. Johanna and J.J. were watching the bees fly in and out of the new hive, while she shared some of the secrets of becoming a successful beekeeper.

Katy was spending the morning at Anna's, playing with her girls, and Jonah perched a few yards away on the bank of the pond. He held a homemade willow-branch fishing pole and was concentrating on his bobber. The cork danced tantalizingly, but whenever he snatched on the line, nothing came up but an empty hook. "They keep stealing my bait, *Mam,*" Jonah protested. "I've only got two worms left." He sighed heavily. "I'll bet it's just sunnies. I don't think there are any big fish in here."

"*Ya,* there are," J.J. insisted. "*Dat* put baby bass in there a long time ago. Once he caught one this big!" He stretched his arms apart to show what Johanna thought must be an exaggerated size, even for a largemouth bass.

"I'm tired of fishing anyway." Jonah dropped the fishing pole onto the grass. "I'm thirsty."

"If you don't want to fish anymore today, put those worms back in the garden," Johanna instructed.

"*Mam,* I'm hot," Jonah whined. "They're just worms."

"The Lord made them as He made you," she said firmly, rising to her feet. "Wrap up your line and fasten that hook so you don't lose an eye. And take the worms back where you dug them. Now." She tugged the brim of her son's hat down. "And your hat will do you no good if it doesn't shade your face from the sun."

"Do we have to leave?" J.J. asked. "I like watching the bees."

"We do. I'm glad you're learning about the bees, but it's time we finished up our chores here and got back home."

Today wasn't Roland's regular day at the horse farm, but someone had stopped by and asked him to replace a shoe on a three-year-old that was scheduled to race. He'd brought J.J. to *Mam's* at 9:00 a.m. and asked Johanna if she could possibly watch J.J. for him. Naturally, she said she'd be glad to help. Roland was grateful, and it really was no trouble. She hadn't planned much for the day, other than to help prepare food for Sunday. And J.J. was a sweet child, not nearly as mischievous as her Jonah. Since she'd been coming to Roland's to tend this new hive, she'd been delighted to find J.J. so interested. She suspected that her earlier conclusions were true—Roland's boy had a real love for bees and a God-given gift for understanding them.

Even if J.J. hadn't shared her interest in bees, Johanna knew her heart would have gone out to him, as a poor motherless child. He had a father who loved him dearly, but the boy desperately missed his mother. He'd been young when Roland's wife had died of complications of diabetes, but he had been able to talk. Roland said that for months, his son had asked for his *mam* and cried out for her in his sleep.

Nighttime, according to Roland, was still a difficult time for them both. J.J., easy in daylight, became fearful and needy once the sun went down. He often woke screaming from nightmares that he couldn't remember. And now, by the way he followed her and clung to her skirt, J.J. was forming an attachment to her. She would have welcomed it, if she'd known for certain that she would become his mother. Another child would fit easily into her arms. But she was afraid that if she and Roland didn't wed, J.J. would be hurt again. And this time, who knew how deeply the boy would be affected.

Johanna never used to think about the complications of relationships. Maybe living with Wilmer and seeing the results of a troubled mind every day had made her more sympathetic to the emotional needs of her family and those around her. Before she'd married, she'd often been impatient with what she felt was weakness, and she'd been inclined to tell those afflicted to "just snap out of it." But, no more. J.J. was wounded. He didn't have a broken arm that could be seen and easily mended. He had suffered a blow to his spirit.

It was true that Katy and Jonah had both lost their father when Wilmer took his own life. But, although Katy had adored her father, there had always been a distance between Wilmer and Jonah. Her son had often been the victim of his father's outbursts, and no amount of persuading on her part had been able to soften Wilmer's verbal attacks on the boy. Strangely, Wilmer's death had caused Jonah's personality to blossom. In weeks, she'd seen her little boy gain self-confidence. He'd begun to speak up, to try new tasks. As perverse as it seemed, Wilmer's absence had brought happiness into Jonah's life. As for Katy, nothing could squelch her merry spirit. She accepted life as it came and enjoyed every moment of every day.

At first, Johanna had worried that having J.J. spend so much time with them, as he had been lately, might spark jealousy. She'd watched Jonah carefully, afraid that he might not like sharing his mother with another boy. But what she'd feared hadn't happened. Instead, Jonah fell into the role of big brother, and J.J. became the faithful pal.

There wasn't much difference in the boys' ages, but she'd tried to raise her children in the way that she'd been reared. Her parents had encouraged her and her sisters to be independent and to believe in their own ability to solve problems and be of help to the family. J.J.'s mother, Pauline, had kept him close, protecting—perhaps overprotecting—him and treating him as if he was younger than he really was. It had been a source of friction between Roland and his wife until her death, and something so obvious that others in the community, including Johanna and her sisters, had remarked on it.

Since Roland had become J.J.'s sole parent, both had had to make adjustments. As far as Johanna could see, Roland was a wonderful father, but it was obvious that he sometimes felt out of his depth. Children needed both a mother and a father. *Mam* was right. Roland needed to take another wife, and soon. She could be that wife...if only she could ease the uncertainty in her mind and her heart.

And she and Roland *were* courting.

He had pointed out the truth of that simple statement last Wednesday and, against her will, she'd had to admit that Roland was right. But she was still no closer to a decision on marriage. She'd enjoyed the day at the beach, even enjoyed kissing Roland more than she felt was decent, but she still felt so uncertain. Courting was a carefree time, a time for a boy and girl to learn more about each other and to learn to be at ease in each other's company. But Roland was no stranger to her. She knew his strengths and his weaknesses. And, more importantly, she knew her own. So their courting was something different. For her, it was about whether or not she wanted to marry again.

Once she made a choice to marry Roland or to remain a widow, she would live with it. She'd already proved with Wilmer that she was capable of dealing with even the most difficult situations. But did she want to? Wasn't it easier to simply step away from remarriage and build a life caring for her son and daughter, and helping her mother with dear Susanna? Wouldn't God approve of that sacrifice? Her sister Ruth had once believed that singleness was the path the Lord had planned for her. But what if it wasn't Ruth who was supposed to serve in that way? What if it was her?

Johanna had been praying for an answer every morning when she woke, and every night before she went to sleep. "Please, Lord, tell me what to do," she pleaded. "Tell me what's right for me, for Roland, for Katy and J.J. and Jonah. Give me the wisdom to know what you want of me."

"*Mam,* I'm hungry."

Jonah's voice interrupted her reverie. "We'll go to Aunt Anna's," she said. "She asked us to take the noon meal with her. Fried chicken and biscuits."

"And blackberry pie," J.J. said, reaching up to clasp Johanna's hand. "Pie is my favorite."

Johanna nodded. Feeding hungry children was something she knew how to do. Johanna had made four loaves of raisin bread early that morning. She'd brought one loaf and a quart of *Mam's* chicken-corn soup and put them in Roland's refrigerator for them to have for that evening's supper. Whether or not she decided to become Roland's wife and J.J.'s mother, they still had to eat. Hadn't *Mam* taught her that looking after neighbors was the right thing to do? Even *Mam* couldn't suggest that she was leading Roland on by seeing that he and his son didn't go without. Or could she?

Johanna was still asking that same question on Sunday when she sat on the bench between Miriam and Aunt Jezzy, and Uncle Reuben asked everyone to stand for "'S Lobg-sang," a slow, traditional hymn that was always sung by the congregation at service. Her mind should have been on the song of praise, but instead, she kept thinking back over the past week.

Thursday night, Roland had come to take her for a drive. They'd left the three children with *Mam,* Rebecca, Grace and Susanna, and they'd gone for pizza and come home the long way. She and Roland had laughed and talked. He'd made no attempt to hold her hand again, and she hadn't tried to kiss him, but she had wondered if he wanted to kiss her. And if he hadn't wanted to…why not? Did it mean that he'd thought she was forward when she'd kissed him at the inlet?

If she leaned a little closer to Aunt Jezzy, she could see Roland standing in the second row behind Anna's Samuel. He'd trimmed his beard that morning, but he needed a haircut. His hair hung over his eyes, and he kept brushing it out of the way. She wondered why his sister Mary hadn't said something about it. It was endless, the list of things that a man living alone with a small boy forgot to do for himself. Maybe she should offer to cut it for him…. She'd trimmed J.J.'s yesterday afternoon when she'd done Jonah's. But it wasn't really fitting for her to cut Roland's hair. That was a little too intimate for comfort. She would suggest that Mary or his mother cut it.

Johanna forced herself to look straight ahead, but she couldn't keep thoughts of Roland out of her head. She could pick out his rich baritone among all the other men. He had a good, strong singing voice, and he never slurred the words to the old songs as some of the younger fellows did. Roland knew all the lyrics, and he could carry the tune, no matter how slow.

She was listening so hard to Roland that she nearly missed a note herself. Miriam cut her eyes at her and suppressed a smile. Johanna averted her gaze, and when she looked up, saw that her aunt Martha, seated just in the next row, had turned to scowl at her. Was it that obvious to everyone that she hadn't been paying attention—that her mind had been on Roland instead of the service? Embarrassed, Johanna gripped the *Ausbund,* the hymnbook, tighter and let her voice blend with the women around her.

When the hymn ended and Preacher Perry began to tell how the Pharaoh's daughter sent her servants to fetch a floating basket from the river, Johanna forced herself to listen to the familiar story of Baby Moses and how he was saved and grew up in the palace as an Egyptian prince. It was a tale she'd always loved, and one Hannah had elaborated on when Johanna was small. *The princess loved the baby as her own, Mam* had said, *just as I love you, and you, and you*...pointing out each of them in turn.

Perry Hershberger was a good speaker and a much-loved preacher, but he suffered from poor health, and his voice was often weak. Today, he seemed better than he had been in many weeks, and Johanna had no trouble following his sermon. His sermons were never as wordy or as dull as Uncle Reuben's, and Preacher Perry usually recited the Bible passages in Low German, not the High German that most preachers favored. Usually, Johanna loved it when he spoke, but today, her mind kept wandering.

Lydia and Norman, this Sunday's hosts, had thrown open the windows to catch the breeze, and fresh air wafted in from outside, making the crowded rooms comfortable for a summer's day. The rest of the service passed quickly, and the next time the congregation rose for a hymn, Johanna kept herself from seeking out Roland Byler with her eyes and making a complete fool of herself.

Bishop Atlee finished with a prayer, and then Samuel, who was deacon, got to his feet to deliver the announcements for the week. Johanna's thoughts drifted again as the bishop asked for remembrance for those who were ill and reminded the community that the next service would be at Aunt Martha and Uncle Reuben's house. He asked for volunteers to paint the Coblentz barn, and then cleared his throat. "Banns are read for couples Menno Swartzentruber and Susie Raber. That's Susie Raber of Swan Creek, Missouri. I think some of you met the John Rabers last year when they came for Wilmer's funeral."

Johanna remembered Ethel Raber, John's wife, but which of her three daughters was Susie? Johanna hadn't heard that Menno was getting married, but that wasn't unusual. Many Amish couples preferred to keep their plans secret until the coming nuptials were announced in church.

She wondered when the bride-to-be and Menno had met and courted, or if theirs was an arranged marriage, as some were. It happened here occasionally, more so out in the Western states, but she'd heard that such unions, typically arranged by parents, usually turned out well. It certainly wouldn't have suited her. At least she'd known Wilmer and had no one else to blame for the disaster of her marriage but herself.

"And first banns called for Naphtali Hilty of District 4, here in Kent County, and our own Jezebel Miller."

Miriam elbowed Johanna as a wave of murmurs rippled through the congregation. Johanna blinked and mouthed silently to her sister, *What? Who?*

"Say that again, Samuel," Noodle Troyer urged from the far corner of the men's benches. "Did you say Jezebel Miller?"

Samuel reddened and cleared his throat again. "Banns called for Naphtali—that's *Nip* Hilty—and *Jezzy* Miller."

Johanna turned to stare at Aunt Jezzy. "Are you… You aren't…"

Aunt Jezzy didn't answer. She just sat primly on her seat, the faintest smile on her lips, one toe tapping the floor, and turned her hymnbook in a circle, very slowly, precisely three times.

"Can I drive you home?" Roland stood by the back porch, waiting as Johanna came down the steps with a market basket full of empty dishes in one hand. It was late afternoon, the Sunday communal meal had been served, the last prayers had been said and the women had cleaned up. Most of the families had already left to do their evening chores.

"The children and I came with *Mam* and Susanna and Rebecca, in our buggy," Johanna answered.

"I know, but J.J. and I want to take you home. He gets bored riding only with his *dat,* don't you, son?" He jiggled the brim of J.J.'s hat.

"Can we, *Mam?*" Katy asked, tugging on her skirt. "Can we ride with Roland and J.J.? Please, can we?"

Jonah had already gone ahead with Charley and

Miriam. Charley had promised Jonah that he'd let him help feed the horses.

Roland looked at her expectantly, and she nodded. What did it matter if people saw them leaving together? Dorcas, *Grossmama* and two other women had already asked her after services if she and Roland were courting. It was being talked about all over the community. Grace called it the Amish Skype. How had Grace put it? *For people who don't have phones or internet service, you can pass news faster than NBC.* Johanna wasn't certain what Skype was or how it worked, but she wasn't about to admit that to Grace.

"J.J. and Katy can act as chaperones," Roland teased as Johanna climbed up into his buggy. Secretly, she was pleased that Roland had asked her to ride with him. You couldn't get much more respectable than riding home from services with a beau.

"Did you know about your aunt and Nip?" Roland flicked the leathers over his gelding's back. "Walk on," he ordered, and the standard-bred started out at a brisk walk and then flowed smoothly into a steady pace.

"*Ne.* It was a total surprise to me. None of us expected her to ever marry."

"She'll make him a good wife. I imagine he's lonely. It's hard for a married man to suddenly be alone. A house feels empty without a woman's footsteps."

Behind them the two children giggled and wiggled, standing up to peer out at other buggies through the small window at the back of the vehicle.

"I'm sorry to hear about your brother-in-law," Roland continued. "Daniel."

The Saturday mail delivery had brought *Mam* a letter from Leah telling that her husband had suffered a relapse of the fever that had plagued him on and off during the rainy season. They had traveled to the city nearest to their mission, where Daniel had received first-rate care. He was expected to make a full recovery, but Leah had asked for prayers from her family. Samuel had taken the request further, and had asked the bishop to lead the congregation in prayer for Daniel's health.

"I worry about Leah, so far away with a baby. It could easily have been one of them who fell ill. Who knows what kinds of fever they have in the jungle? It was kind of Bishop Atlee to ask for everyone to remember Daniel in their devotions. Some bishops wouldn't be so understanding… since Leah left our faith to become Mennonite."

"Bishop Atlee is a kind man, one who truly walks in God's ways, as much as he can." Her hand rested on the bench seat, and Roland laid his lightly on top of it. "You must miss her a lot. I can't imagine being that far from Charley or Mary."

"I do miss her," Johanna agreed.

The buggy wheels and the horse's hooves made a comforting sound as they struck the road. *Sounds of home,* Johanna thought. And she wondered what strange sounds Leah heard in the Brazilian jungle.

"J.J. and I appreciated the soup and the raisin bread," Roland said. "Especially the raisin bread. We finished it up for breakfast this morning, all but three slices."

Johanna's eyes widened. "An entire loaf?"

"We were hungry, weren't we, son?"

"Ya, Dat," J.J. agreed. "We were hungry."

"When have you ever *not* been hungry?" Johanna teased. Tenseness drained out of her body, and she found that she was enjoying herself. When Roland wasn't pressing her to give him a decision, she loved being with him. It was almost like old times...maybe even better.

The journey home from Lydia and Norman's didn't take long, but when they came up the Yoder driveway and drove around to the farmyard, the first thing she saw was Charley's open buggy and Miriam's brown-and-white pony, Taffy, hitched to the rail.

"Why are Charley and Miriam here?" Johanna asked. "They didn't leave long before we did." The thought that something might have happened to Jonah occurred to her, and her stomach sank. "I hope—"

"Johanna!" Eli stepped out of the kitchen door. "Ruth's time. It's come."

Johanna was already scrambling down from the buggy. "Get Katy," she called over her shoulder to Roland. "Have you sent someone to call for the midwife?" Johanna asked her brother-in-law. "Where's Ruth? Is she—"

"In the house here," Eli answered. "My wife got it in her head that she wanted the babies to be born here, in the same room where she was born. Miriam's with her."

"Jonah?"

"In the barn. I thought it best to keep him out of the house, so I told him to feed the cows."

Johanna turned to Roland. "Thank you for bringing me home. I have to go to help Ruth." And then to Eli, "The midwife? Has someone sent for her?" Ruth had engaged the services of a midwife affiliated with an obstetrical practice in Dover. They'd planned a home birth from the beginning, but this was the first that Johanna had known that Ruth wanted to have the babies here at their childhood home.

"Charley," Eli answered, sounding a little lost. "Charley went to use the phone at the chair shop."

"How about if I take Jonah home with me?"

Roland offered. "Eli's right. A birthing's no place for a young boy."

"Or a little girl." Johanna thought for a moment. "If you don't mind, take Katy to Fannie and Roman's."

Katy popped her head out of the buggy.

"Would you like that?" Johanna asked. "Would you like to go and play with Fannie's girls?"

"Ya," Katy agreed. Fannie's youngest two were seven and nine, and Katy adored them.

"Don't worry about your children," Roland said. "I'll see to them."

Johanna nodded and hurried toward the house. Ruth had said she was tired that morning and that her back ached. *Mam* had rightfully advised her to stay home from services. "How is she?" Johanna asked Eli. "Is she certain it's her time?"

"She's certain," Eli said. "Her pains are coming regularly and her water broke about an hour ago."

"It sounds as though you're about to become a father," Johanna said, trying to sound cheerful. "I'd appreciate it if you'd see to our animals—the chickens, horses, cows—"

Eli nodded. "Glad to do it. Glad to have something useful to do."

Johanna smiled at him. "It will be all right, Eli. Women have been having babies since the beginning of time. Ruth is a strong woman, and she's in good health. Pray for her, and don't worry."

"I'll pray," Eli promised, "but don't expect me not to worry. That's my Ruth in there."

Chapter Fourteen

Leaving Roland to care for her children, Johanna entered the kitchen and found both Miriam and Ruth standing by the sink. Ruth was filling a tea-kettle. "Are you in labor?" Johanna asked. She took one look at Ruth's strained face and knew that the question was unnecessary. "How often are your contractions?"

"About ten minutes apart." Ruth set the kettle on the counter, leaned against the cabinets and closed her eyes. "They're strong," she admitted softly, "but nothing I can't deal with. I wouldn't have said anything yet if my water hadn't broken." She raised an eyebrow. "Eli's making a fuss for nothing. I'm not going to have these babies for hours."

"I tried to get her into bed." Miriam had her hands on her hips, an expression on her face that was exactly like *Mam's* when she was cross. "But

Ruth wanted peppermint tea and insists on making it herself."

"I can't just sit around and wait. I've been waiting for months." Ruth exhaled slowly and her features relaxed. "There, better now. I'm not sick. I'm just having a baby...babies. *Mam* had seven of us, all born here at home." Her gaze locked with Johanna's, and Johanna saw a flicker of uncertainty. "I didn't want to go to the hospital—to have my babies come into the world in a strange room full of noise and Englishers. Do you think that's silly of me?"

Unconsciously, Ruth crumpled the corner of her apron between her fingers, a habit of hers when she was uncertain. As a young girl, Ruth had chewed the ends of her apron strings ragged, but thankfully, she seemed to have outgrown that. *Mam* had worried that she never would.

Ruth wasn't quite as brave as she lets on, Johanna decided, wondering if Ruth was concerned due to her own difficulty with Jonah's birth. Her son had come too early, and she'd nearly lost him. *"Ne,"* she said soothingly. "I think it makes sense, Ruth. Everything has gone well with you. And your midwife wouldn't have approved a home birth if she wasn't certain everything would go well." Ruth was always uneasy outside of her Amish community, and there was no reason for her to be in the hospital as long as the delivery went smoothly.

"Everyone says that twins come early, but these two are a week overdue. Linda said that if they weren't born soon, she would admit me and have Dr. Sharez induce labor." Ruth made a face. "I didn't want that. It seems unnatural. I always thought they would come in God's time."

"And so they have." Johanna removed her black bonnet and offered Ruth a comforting smile. "Well, I think tea is a good idea. We'd better make a big pot. *Mam,* Susanna and Rebecca will be home soon." She crossed the worn kitchen floor and touched Ruth's cheek. "You can do this, little sister. Look at our Leah. She gave birth to her baby in the jungle, with only Daniel to help her."

"And put it in a hammock," Miriam noted. "Everyone in the house sleeps in a hammock. We did, too, when we were there visiting. You should have seen Charley trying to get the hang of it." She chuckled, and then went on. "Leah said she was afraid to put the baby in a cradle because there are giant ants." She grimaced. "At least Ruth doesn't have to worry about ants."

Ruth put the teakettle on the gas stove and lit the burner. "We sent Charley to call the midwife and I asked him to fetch Anna."

"That's another good reason for coming home to *Mam's* to deliver your precious babies," Johanna said. "*Mam's* house is a lot bigger than yours, and, counting her, the four of us and—"

"Five, counting Grace," Miriam corrected. "Don't forget Grace. She'll be home eventually."

"Five of us, plus Aunt Jezzy. And speaking of Aunt Jezzy..." In the excitement about Ruth's coming childbirth, Johanna had almost forgotten about Aunt Jezzy's surprise announcement. "You are never going to believe it, but Samuel called the banns for her and Nip after services and..."

Ruth chuckled. "Miriam told me. Good for her. I like Nip. He'll take good care of her." She reached up on a shelf and brought down an old tin box with Dutch flowers painted on it. "Peppermint all right with you?"

"I want chamomile," Miriam said and then went on in a rush, "I'm so excited for Aunt Jezzy. She's spent her whole life taking care of *Grossmama*. She deserves to be happy."

"I have to admit, I was shocked." Johanna dangled her bonnet by the strings. She hesitated, and then said what was foremost in her thoughts. "And being happy, if you're a woman, does it always mean marrying?" She sighed. "Never mind me. Forget I asked that." She glanced at Ruth again. "This is a happy time for you, for all of us. Give me a few minutes to change out of my church clothes, and we'll all have that tea before you get too uncomfortable to enjoy it."

"Take your time," Ruth said as she put tea bags into mugs. Another contraction began and she gritted her teeth and rubbed the small of her back. "I'm not going anywhere."

The kitchen door opened and Eli poked his head in. "Ruth, are you all right? Why aren't you in bed?" He glanced at Johanna for confirmation. "Shouldn't she be—?"

"*Ne,* Eli." Ruth went to the door, and touched his hand lightly. "I'm fine," she assured him. "Stop worrying. Surely you must have animals to feed."

Johanna turned away, strangely touched by the tenderness between them. Among her people, public shows of affection, even between husband and wife, were rare. But Ruth and Eli were a lot like *Mam* and *Dat.* They didn't seem to care who saw that they loved each other.

"We'll take good care of her," Johanna called over her shoulder. She didn't want to intrude, but as she walked into the hallway that led to the parlor, she couldn't help hearing Eli's reply.

"I fed them. And I watered them all and forked down hay."

"Then go home and feed Charley's stock and our own," Ruth suggested. "This is no place for a man. This is women's work."

"But I want to do something."

"Pray for our babies," she said.

"And for you, Ruth. I—"

Johanna couldn't hear the rest of what Eli said, but the sense of his caring and his love for her sister brought a catch to her throat. Ruth had found a good man. He made her happy. And if she felt the restraint of being subject to her husband's will, Ruth had never hinted at it by word or action.

Would that Wilmer and I could have had such a relationship, she thought wistfully. He'd been away the night Jonah had come into the world, and he'd only come to the hospital twice, once to pick her up when she was released and again, weeks later, when their tiny son had finally been strong enough to come home. The Amish didn't believe in insurance, as the English did, feeling that paying outsiders to cover unexpected losses showed a lack of faith in the Lord. Her own C-section and Jonah's long stay in the neonatal care unit had saddled them with a heavy debt. And Wilmer had unconsciously blamed Jonah for the burden.

As she climbed the stairs, she reminded herself that life moves on. *Wilmer is dead, gone on to a better place, and God has blessed me with two healthy children.* Today, she had learned that her dear aunt was marrying, and Ruth—after waiting so long—was going to become a mother. Maybe her mother was right. Maybe it was time she put the past behind her and looked to the future… whatever that would be.

The sounds of Susanna's whoop of excitement,

Jeremiah's high-pitched barking and the bustle of more people coming into the house quickened Johanna's step. She promised herself that she wouldn't wallow in her own concerns, but give herself wholeheartedly to Ruth's special day.

In her room, Johanna changed quickly into a clean, everyday work dress and apron. And by the time she got back to the kitchen, she found not only Rebecca, *Mam* and Susanna there, but Anna, Aunt Jezzy and *Grossmama,* as well. Ruth was re-filling the teakettle while Susanna fetched sugar, milk and lemon slices for their grandmother's tea.

"Marrying, at your age." *Grossmama* shook her finger at Aunt Jezzy. "And to a man old enough to be your grandfather. It's indecent."

Aunt Jezzy giggled, blushed and twirled her tea cup. "She doesn't think I'm old enough to get married," she said to Johanna.

Johanna tried not to show her amusement. Aunt Jezzy was *Grossmama's* younger sister but, still, a woman in her sixties. Her grandmother's mind often wandered these days, and her family was usually at odds as whether to laugh or cry at her stubborn declarations...especially the one where she believed *Dat*, *Grossmama's* only son, was still alive and in the barn milking.

"At fifteen?" *Grossmama* exclaimed, insisting that Aunt Jezzy was a teenage girl. "The bishop won't allow it. It's your duty to stay home and help your mother raise the younger children."

Johanna had learned that the easiest way to handle her grandmother was to agree with whatever she said and wait for her to move on to a new topic. The strangest thing was that for much of the time, she was perfectly lucid and had an excellent memory.

Johanna found a seat beside *Grossmama* and slipped an arm around her shoulders. "But Nip will be a good provider," she said. "People order his bridles and halters from all over the country." *Grossmama* frowned, and Johanna went on. "And you married young, yourself, *ne?*"

Grossmama snorted. "And lived to regret it. All those useless girls and only a single son to support me in my old age." She pointed at Anna. "My Jonas's wife. She's a good girl. She's given him two strong sons and this sweet baby girl." She waved a wrinkled finger at tiny Rose, who was now cradled in *Mam's* arms.

Johanna didn't try to explain that Anna was Jonas's daughter and stepmother to Samuel's two boys and three little girls. Baby Rose was Anna and Samuel's child. That part, at least, was true. "But your mother has other girls at home to help her," Johanna said, humoring her grandmother. "Better Jezzy marry her good harness maker before some other *meadle* snatches him up." Johanna hoped God would forgive her for encouraging her *Grossmama's* fancies, but arguing with her just made her worse. And there should be no strife here today with Ruth's babies coming so soon.

"True, true," *Grossmama* agreed. "Jezzy's nothing to look at, and her butter never firms up. I always made the best butter, sweet and salty and yellow as the sun, so my *Dat* always said."

"Your butter is the best," Aunt Jezzy agreed with a twinkle in her eye. "And our Ruthie takes after you." She patted her sister's hand and smiled at Johanna. "And I will be close by if you need anything, just next door."

Johanna tilted her head and her eyes widened in curiosity. "Next door?"

"Ya." Anna joined the conversation. "Nip has bought five acres from Samuel just across the road from our house. He wants to leave his harness shop and house for his second son, Joel, and build a new house for Aunt Jezzy. He thought it might be hard for her to change church districts and leave all of us. So she and Nip will be our new neighbors."

"I never!" Aunt Martha and her daughter Dorcas stood in the open doorway, arms full. "You could have knocked me over with a feather when Samuel cried the banns for Aunt Jezzy and Nip. And him to build her a new house! If we have snow in midsummer or Rebecca married a Quaker, I'd not be more surprised."

"Just a little house." Aunt Jezzy hurried to take the pound cake from Aunt Martha's hands while Dorcas carried a heavy kettle of soup and set it on the stove. "The two of us don't need so much room and Joel will be wanting a wife soon. Best we leave him to it. He's a fine harness maker, Nip says, and walking out with a girl from Belleville. Easier for the young folk to make a start without old folks peering over their shoulders."

"I never," Aunt Martha repeated. "That's more words than I ever heard you string together at one time, and you quiet as mouse about courting Nip." She shook her head and took down a coffee cup. "We've come to help out," she said. "Had a vegetable beef soup warming on the back of the stove and said to Reuben, 'I'll just take that soup and that lemon pound cake to Hannah's. I've sat at many a birthing.'" She offered a tight smile to Ruth. "Sensible for you to have your little ones here. No need for English doctors and hospitals." She threw a glance at Dorcas. "You see that, daughter? Ruth found a good man, and her with red hair and freckles and a tongue in her mouth that won't stop. You could do the same if you'd put your mind to—"

"Am I too late?" Grace said, barely visible under

a sliding tower of pizza boxes, as she came into the kitchen. "Ruth didn't have the babies—"

"Not yet." Ruth rose to her feet and extended her arms to catch a falling pizza. "Didn't you and John have a meeting with your preacher tonight? About your wedding?"

"Daniel's aunt got a call from her cousin Arnie Brown. Noodle Troyer said you were in labor. Pizza Tonight messed up the order for our adult evening Sunday-school class and brought us double. The minister said there'd be a lot of people here, and Hannah shouldn't have to cook and I should just bring the extra pizzas." Grace dumped four boxes on the counter. "Are you really going to have the babies here?" Grace demanded. "Tonight?" She looked around. "With all of us here?"

Ruth chuckled. "I hope we'll have them tonight. And this is just what I want. My family—"

A car horn sounded outside, and Johanna leaned back to push aside the curtain and peer out. A blue sedan with a stork decal on the door was just pulling up to the fence. "There's the midwife," Johanna said. "But there's another woman with her."

"That's the RN, Jennifer Bryant," Ruth answered. "She's... Ohhh." She gasped. "That's a strong one."

"Good." Johanna clasped her hands together. "I guess that means we're going to have these babies sooner rather than later."

* * *

As Johanna had predicted, Ruth's labor and delivery went as smoothly as possible. Red-haired Adam, six pounds and fourteen ounces, slid into the midwife's hands at 5:43 a.m., followed only twenty-one minutes later by blond and chubby Luke, who outweighed his older brother by five ounces. Both boys had dark blue eyes and fair complexions. Other than hair color, they seemed as identical and content as two peas in a pod as they stared with wide-eyed innocence as joyous women gathered to welcome them into the world.

By ten o'clock that morning, the nurse and the midwife had given final instructions and gone, promising to return several times over the coming week. Aunt Martha and Dorcas had driven *Grossmama,* Anna and Rose home, and Aunt Jezzy had gone to take a nap. Ruth and Eli were sharing tea and slices of blueberry pie at *Mam's* table while Irwin admired the new babies.

"They're so small," Irwin said. "They have little fingers and noses."

"Ya," Susanna agreed. "Little noses." She giggled. "King David and me. We're getting married. Having two babies." Her round face beamed. "Girl babies."

"Not anytime soon, I hope," *Mam* said. "Now, be a big help to me, and you and Irwin go feed the chickens."

Johanna sat in Aunt Jezzy's rocker with Luke while Eli cradled Adam in the crook of his arm. She looked down at Luke. Had her own felt this sweet in her arms…been this tiny and perfect? She knew that Jonah had been even smaller, but it was easy to forget the softness of a newborn's skin and the scent of a clean baby.

Adam was fast asleep, but Luke's eyes were open, his pink lips pursed and dribbling a few drops of milk. Ruth had dressed the boys in pale blue cotton gowns, long-sleeved, that tied at the bottom. White, tight-fitting caps covered their heads, but ringlets peeped out at the forehead and cheeks.

"I'm surprised they have so much hair," Eli said.

Ruth smiled and her weary but happy gaze met Johanna's. Ruth's face was pale, but other than the shadows under her eyes, she hardly looked like a woman who'd stayed awake all night and delivered twins. The nurse had urged her to try to get some sleep, but Ruth insisted on getting up and coming to the kitchen for breakfast.

Johanna had been concerned, but *Mam* wasn't.

"I was exactly the same way," *Mam* pronounced. "When the house quiets down and the excitement wears off, they can all three sleep."

"Mam!" Miriam called from the pantry. "Where's the detergent?" She and Rebecca had volunteered to do the Monday wash.

"There a new box behind... Never mind, I'll find it," *Mam* answered, rising to her feet. On her way out of the kitchen, she stopped to gaze down at the baby in Johanna's arms. "The Lord has blessed you and Eli," she said to Ruth. "Now comes the hard part, raising them to be men like Eli and my Jonas."

"We'll do our best," Ruth promised, stroking Adam's cheek. Then she glanced over at Johanna. "I can't believe they're here. I can't believe..."

"There was ever a time without them," Johanna finished for her. She tucked her index finger into Luke's hand and he tightened his grip around it. A flood of emotion brought tears to Johanna's eyes.

She gathered Luke in her arms and cradled him against her shoulder. He wiggled and made small baby noises that tugged at her heart. *I need another baby.* And suddenly, all the doubts about remarrying that had troubled her for months dissolved away into nothing. Family was what was important. And if she wanted more children, she would have to marry. "I have to go and see Roland," she said abruptly.

Ruth chuckled. "It's about time." She looked at Eli, whose expression was blank. "Poor Roland. He doesn't know it, but his single days are numbered."

Eli glanced at Johanna. "You Yoder girls... Do you have any idea what's she's talking about?"

Johanna didn't answer. She passed sweet Luke to *Mam,* grabbed a scarf off the peg by the door and tied it over her hair as she hurried out the door.

"Where are you off to in such a hurry?" her mother called after her.

"Roland's!" Johanna's heart pounded in her chest. She crossed the yard, nearly colliding with Irwin, who was coming out of the barn. "Could you hitch Blackie for me?" she said. "To *Dat's* courting buggy."

"Now?" Irwin grimaced and reached up to scratch a mosquito bite on his arm. "Jonas's courting buggy? There's two bags of feed sitting in front of—"

"That's the carriage I want," she said. "I need the courting buggy. It's past time I found a husband."

Chapter Fifteen

Johanna drove Blackie at a fast trot down the lane toward the blacktop. She knew she was being impulsive, but she couldn't help herself. She'd always been that way; once she made up her mind on something, she had to do something about it. And she was going to do something about her and Roland.

She'd had enough courting. What woman her age courted, anyway? If Roland wanted to marry her, as he said he did, it was time. They were a well-matched couple. They had grown up with the same values and the same customs and friends. Despite what had happened before between them when they were teens, she knew the measure of Roland as a man. She could give herself entirely to the partnership with him without fear that he would be unkind to her children or fail to provide for them.

It had been difficult and had required many hours of prayer and many tears, but gradually, she had forgiven Wilmer for his weaknesses... for his illness. She was not so much locking the gate on that part of her life, but opening a window to let in the fresh air of spring after a long, dark winter. Wilmer was in God's care, and it was not her place to judge Wilmer or to speak ill to Jonas and Katy of their father. Instead, she had sought diligently for something honest she could tell them and found a gentle truth. *Wilmer was a man who spent his lifetime seeking God and struggling with his own human failures to live according to the faith.* That should give both her children a sense of satisfaction and hope that the Lord would consider his sickness and take pity on him.

"I'll not make the mistakes I made with Wilmer," Johanna said aloud. Blackie heard her and perked up his ears. She reined him to a halt as they neared the road and looked both ways to see that no traffic was coming. Then she flicked the leathers over his back to guide him out onto the shoulder that bordered the high-crowned blacktop.

"I'll curb my willful nature," she pronounced, more to herself than to the horse. Blackie tossed his head, but whether he agreed or disagreed or was simply shaking off a horsefly, she didn't know. Her thoughts were now flying in so many directions...life was so full of possibilities.

From the first day she exchanged vows with Roland, she would put aside her own selfish needs. She would be more like Anna, making an effort to curb her stubbornness and to remember that her husband was ordained by God to be the head of the family. Not that she wouldn't speak up, but she'd allow herself to be guided by her husband.

In return, she would have her own house again. J.J., Jonah and Katy would have both a mother and a father, and she and Roland could work together to teach all three of them, bringing them up to be good and productive members of the community. Her fears that she would be a burden on her mother would vanish, and she would have the pleasure of cleaning and reorganizing Roland's home from top to bottom. And, God willing, she and Roland would be blessed by more children… her own sweet babies to cuddle and care for.

By the time she turned into Roland's lane, Johanna's spirits were high. It had always been that way for her. She would struggle for days or weeks with a decision, but once it had been made, she threw herself into whatever it was wholeheartedly. "How do you like this barnyard?" she asked Blackie. "And the stable? It looks comfortable to me. Maybe you'll be living here soon." She couldn't help but smile at her own silliness in talking to a horse as if it understood. If anyone heard her, they'd think she'd been eating too much May butter and was addled.

It was a good place, this farm of Roland's. It pleased Johanna to see the buildings tidy, the roofs sound, the siding and concrete block walls painted red with white trim, the doors hanging straight, with no sagging. Likewise, the windmill—blades turning regularly in the wind—seemed as solid and substantial as the rest of the outbuildings. It was evident that Roland was a hard worker, a man who believed in keeping his barn and sheds and house in shape.

She reined in Blackie near the hitching rail and gave a sigh of relief to see that Roland's buggy was still in the open shed.

Her gaze fell on a bare patch at the back of the house. There was a low brick wall running around it, telling Johanna that someone had once planted flowers there. It would be a good spot for climbing roses, she thought. She'd always favored red roses, the old-fashioned kind that took the heat well and thrived with only a little care. She could imagine the way the air would smell early in the morning, and decided that when she came to be the wife in this house, she would plant flowers everywhere.

At that instant, Jonah and J.J. came running around the chicken coop. Jonah was in front, and he had lengths of baling twine tied to each arm. J.J. was behind him, holding the strings as though they were reins. When he caught sight of her, J.J. stopped short and dropped the reins onto the ground.

Jonah snorted like a horse, jumped into the air, and then saw her and began to giggle. *"Mam!"* he cried and ran up and hugged her. "J.J. has a cart, like a wagon, but with two wheels. We were playing horse and…and… Are my baby cousins—did they come last night?"

"Early this morning." She squeezed him tightly. "Good morning, J.J.," she said with a smile, and then went on about the babies. "Two little boys, Adam and Luke, one with yellow hair and one with ginger."

"Like me!"

"Like you," she agreed. "It looks like you two are having fun. I hope you helped Roland with chores this morning." She looked around but didn't see him. "Is J.J.'s father in the house?"

The back door opened and Roland's sister Mary stepped out. "Morning!" she called. "Did everything go well with Ruth?"

"It did, God be thanked. The babies are healthy and Ruth is already up and on her feet." Johanna straightened Jonah's straw hat. "Go and play while you can," she said. "We'll be going home soon."

"I get to be the horse next," J.J. called.

"All right." Jonah nodded. "But first you have

to catch me!" With that, he darted off, J.J. shrieking merrily and scampering after him.

"I've just made a fresh pot of coffee," Mary said, "and corn muffins for the boys. Would you like to come in and have some? It seems so long since we've had time for a good chat."

Johanna hesitated. She liked Mary, considered her one of her good friends, and she always enjoyed visiting with her, but today... Johanna swallowed, trying to ease the tightness in her throat. "Actually," she admitted, "I've come to talk to Roland."

"He's not here," Mary answered. "I'm sorry, but he was called to his new job at Windward Farms. John Hartman picked him up early this morning. That's why I'm here with the boys." Mary's expression showed her concern. "I hope it's nothing bad," she said.

Johanna's stomach clenched. "He's not here? But I thought... I saw his buggy and..." Mary's words sank in. John had picked him up. *Roland wasn't here.* She'd gotten her nerve up and come to say her piece, and it was all for nothing.

"I hope whatever it is..." Mary brought a hand to her mouth, clearly torn between wanting to know what was so important between them and not wanting to seem nosy. "You two..." She took a deep breath and went on in a rush. "I hope that your courting...you know what I mean." She flushed. "I guess what I'm trying to say is that I'd love to have you as my sister...if..."

Johanna smiled. "You know I can think of no one I'd rather have for a new sister than you."

"Sorry you missed him. I don't know how long before he'll be home." She motioned toward the direction the boys had gone. "Anyway, J.J. and Jonah are having such a good time, would you care if your boy stayed here? I can get my driver to drop him off at the house when I go home. It was short notice." She chuckled. "Roland sent John for me this morning after he got word he was needed. It's a wonder John gets any vet business done, what with all his running around, driving the Amish."

Johanna felt the energy drain out of her. Suddenly, the strain of being up all night without sleep began to sink in. If she couldn't speak to Roland this morning, she wondered if she'd have the nerve to try again tomorrow. "You don't mind watching Jonah?" she asked. "Are you sure you don't mind?"

"Ne." Mary opened the screen door wider to let a striped tabby cat walk into the kitchen. "Not at all. Jonah is always good for me. Helpful and well mannered."

Johanna grimaced. "Better here than at home, I suppose. Sometimes, he can be a handful."

"Natural for boys," Mary said. "You should see some of my cousins' kids. But Jonah will be a help. I've got some string beans for them to snap after their lunch, and eggs to gather, but mostly they can play. J.J. gets lonely here all by himself. I'm glad he has a chance to be with Jonah today."

"If you're sure…" Johanna glanced back at the hitching rail where Blackie waited. "He's at Windward, you say. That isn't far. I think…" Suddenly, she remembered that she'd come away from the house in just her old blue scarf, not fitting to be seen by English or by strangers on the road. She didn't want to shame herself or Roland. But Mary was wearing her starched white *Kapp*…

"Mary? Could I borrow your prayer *Kapp* and bonnet?"

"My *Kapp* and bonnet? Of course, but…sure." She went back into the house and returned in less than a minute with her black bonnet. "Why do you need it?" But she was already removing the pins that held her *Kapp* in place.

"I'm going to find Roland," Johanna said, trading her worn scarf for Mary's *Kapp* and bonnet. "What I need to say, I have to say now, and if it means following him to his work, I'll have to do it."

"If it's so important, you should go," Mary encouraged.

Johanna thought she read admiration mixed with curiosity in Mary's eyes. "Roland may be shocked to see me there, but I only need to talk to him for a few minutes," she said, more to convince herself than Mary. "It's just that this can't wait."

"Ya," Mary agreed. Then, impulsively, she hugged Johanna and kissed her cheek. "Be careful out on the roads among the English," she cautioned. "I can't have anything happen to my new sister-to-be."

Johanna tied Mary's bonnet over the white *Kapp* and hurried toward her buggy. She hoped Roland wouldn't be angry to see her at his place of work, but if his first reaction was disapproval, maybe he'd change his mind once he heard what she had to say. And now that she'd made up her mind, she had to get it out or burst.

Mary waved as Johanna untied Blackie, got into the buggy and turned around in the yard. "Good luck!" Mary called.

"Thanks," Johanna replied, heart racing. "I'll need it."

Roland, accompanied by John Hartman, approached one of the main paddocks at Windward Farms, where a trainer was working with a yearling colt. "That's Sea You Later, out of Seaside Belle," John said, pointing to the bay colt Rodney Dale was lunging. "You wouldn't believe how much they paid for him."

"You're right," Roland agreed with a grin. "I probably wouldn't."

He liked John, and he was glad he'd been there today to ease the awkwardness of meeting the trainer and grooms that he hadn't had an opportunity to meet before. Usually, Roland was fine around the English, but horsemen could be difficult. He had to gain their respect by doing a good job with their animals. And some of the horses were worth more than he made in a year.

Still, horses were horses, and he knew horses. He'd learned his skills from an uncle, and he was still learning. John had been headed to Windward Farms to give some vaccinations, and he'd offered to give Roland a ride there, and promised to stop back later in the day to take him home.

John, a local veterinarian, was betrothed to Johanna's half sister Grace, and if his own marriage went off with Johanna, as Roland hoped, he and John would be brothers-in-law. For all his education, John didn't seem as English as the others did to Roland. Of course, John was Mennonite, and the Amish and the Mennonite shared history and beliefs. John might not have been born in Kent County, but he fit in well here, and was well liked by the Amish and English farmers and horsemen alike. Roland was pleased to count John as a friend, and John seemed to return the sentiment.

The trainer brought the young horse to a halt and waved Roland and John into the paddock. "I wanted you to check out his hooves," Rodney said. "I think there's a crack in—" He stopped and looked past the two men. "Don't see that often around here."

Roland turned to see Johanna in the Yoder buggy pull in front of the barn, and he walked quickly toward her. His first thought was that something had happened to J.J., and a band tightened around his chest. "Johanna?" he called. "Are the boys all right?" He went to her and placed a hand on the dashboard.

"Our boys are fine. With Mary," Johanna insisted. "And Ruth was delivered of two healthy sons. She's good, as well."

Confusion made his voice sharper than he intended. "Then why—"

"I know this is not the place," she said, glancing at the other men, then back at him. "But it is the time. And if I didn't come now, I might not have had the courage to say this again. Please, Roland." She clutched at his arm. "We need to talk. Privately."

"All right." He nodded and glanced back to where John and Rodney waited. "I'll just be a minute," he shouted to them.

John raised a hand in acknowledgment.

Roland cleared his throat. "Say what you've come to say, then, Johanna." His first thought was *I'm going to lose her.* He wanted to cover his ears and shout, anything to block out the words that would mean it was over between them. "But you do know that I love you," he managed. "That I've never stopped loving you."

"Roland…" she began.

"Ne." He held up a hand. "It's true, God help me. I married a good woman, respected her, cared for her, honored her. But secretly, in my heart, I've always held a place for you, Johanna." He swallowed, trying to rid his mouth of the taste of ashes. "I promise you, if you'll give me the chance, you'll never find another man who will cherish and care for you and your children as I will."

"Will you stop talking for just one minute," she said, "and let me speak my piece?" Tears filled her eyes and spilled over, catching the sunlight and sparkling on her freckled cheeks. "I'm not breaking up with you, *dummkopf.* I want you to ask Samuel to read our banns at the next service. I've done all you asked of me, and I think we should stop all this game-playing and marry. As soon as permitted."

The ground shifted under him. He couldn't catch his breath. She wanted him—wanted to marry him. She loved him as he loved her. He wasn't losing her after all. "Johanna…I…" He looked into her eyes, and a chill seeped through his rising joy. "Marry now?" he asked.

"Ya, marry now, or stop seeing each other altogether." Her chin firmed. "If you want me to be your wife, you need to make a decision."

A part of him wanted to pull her out of the buggy and swing her in his arms. *They could be married!*

But a part of him was immediately suspicious. He knew Johanna well and this was not like her—to come here declaring her love. "Why now? Why are you saying this here…today?" he asked, searching her beautiful face. "Have your feelings about me changed from last time we talked about this?"

Her gaze shifted, no longer meeting his, and Roland felt his hopes sink. *Let it go. Take her hand, tell her you'll have the banns read next Sunday and be thankful for what you have.* But he couldn't do that.

"Do you love me, Johanna?" He leaned closer to her, looking up into her face. "Truly love me?"

She hesitated and when she spoke again, her voice took on a stubborn tone. "Why does that matter?"

"It matters to *me*."

She hesitated, then shifted her gaze to his again. "Do you want me to lie to you?" Now he heard anger in her voice. "I loved you once, and you broke my heart. I won't do that again, Roland. I can't. I'll marry you and give you all that's due a husband, but don't ask for love, Roland, because I don't have it to give."

Chapter Sixteen

Roland's face went gray, and for an instant, Johanna wished she could take back the words. She didn't want to cause him pain—but would it be fair to go into a marriage without being honest? "Roland," she began in a softer voice. "I don't—"

"*Ne.*" His jawline went rigid. The lines of his face grew taut, and beneath his worn blue shirt, farrier's muscles knotted and strained against the thin fabric.

He needs someone to sew him a new shirt. The notion came swiftly and unbidden, even as the passion in his voice pierced her thoughts.

"*Ne.* It won't be like that," he said. "I won't allow your foolish pride to ruin what we could have together."

"Pride?" The sharpness of the accusation stung with a black wasp's venom. "I'll admit to a stubborn nature," she replied, looking down at him from her perch on the buggy seat, "but you can't accuse me of *Hochmut*." The sin of pride was a major fault in the followers of her faith, and to have Roland think it of her—let alone speak it aloud—was an insult.

"I do accuse you of pride. And of being judgmental."

"I'm not," she protested, cheeks burning. "How can you say such a thing?"

"Who was the one who set her mind against Grace? Who refused to give her a chance—who didn't want to accept her as the sister she is to you now?"

A metallic taste spread across the roof of Johanna's mouth. *"Ya,"* she admitted grudgingly. "I was uncharitable toward Grace, at first, but it was to protect *Mam*."

Roland was quiet.

Her stomach clenched and she felt the sting of tears on the inside of her eyelids. Whether the tears were anger or regret, she didn't know. "I apologized to Grace, and told her I was wrong. I'm just slow to come around sometimes. Even Anna thinks we share *Grossmama* Yoder's stubborn streak."

Roland glanced toward the ring where the two men waited and then turned his attention back to her. "I never held your stubborn nature against you," he said. "I've always admired it. What I'm saying is that it's your pride that's the problem. And if you can't see it when it's staring you in the face, there's no chance for us."

Johanna recoiled. "How is it pride to remember that you betrayed me? Betrayed the promises we'd made to each other?"

A dark flush washed over his chiseled features. "We were young, Johanna. I was young and foolish, and I let Emma Mae Troyer kiss me." He threw up his hands. "I shouldn't have let it happen, but honestly—"

"I don't want to hear it." Johanna grabbed for the reins, but Roland was quicker. He clasped them tightly in one hand and seized her hand with the other. She tried to pull away, but he held on to her.

"You will listen," he said quietly, but firmly. "If you never speak a word to me again, you will hear me out." His mouth tightened into a thin line, and his hard gaze penetrated hers.

Johanna felt goose bumps rise on her arms. Never in his life had Roland spoken to her in this tone. And yet, even as she wanted to contest what he was saying, she wasn't in the least frightened— not as she had been when Wilmer had been in one of his rages.

She began to wish she hadn't come here…that she hadn't given in to her impulsiveness. She should have just waited and approached Roland that evening at home. This certainly wasn't how she meant this to turn out.

"It was a harvest party. At Saul Beachy's farm."

"I've heard all I want to hear about you and Emma Mae Troyer—enough to last me a lifetime."

Roland released her hand. "You need to listen to me," he said. "Please listen."

She tucked her hand under her apron, trying to shake off the warmth of his touch, trying to deny that some small part of her had wanted him to go on holding her. She stared straight ahead. "I'm listening."

"Some of the older fellows, my cousin Al and some of his buddies, had bought beer," Roland said. "Two of the English girls were drinking, too. I didn't see any Amish girls drink alcohol, but you know how the young people are up there. Most of the Lancaster communities allow *Rumspringa*. Some kids behave badly before they settle down and join the church."

"And you?" she flung at him. "You didn't see that it was wrong?"

"I didn't drink any of the beer."

"But you didn't leave, either, did you? You knew we were going to get married, but you didn't care if you shamed me by taking part in such a gathering?"

"It was just a barn frolic. We were bringing in shocks and husking corn. Al brought a radio and everyone was listening to the music." He swallowed, and she saw uncertainty cloud his eyes. "It was exciting," Roland admitted. "We were just joking around, having fun. Some people were dancing. I knew it wasn't something my father would approve of, but I didn't know how to get out of it and not feel embarrassed. I'd come with Al, and I knew that if I hitched a ride home to my uncle's, he'd want to know where Al was."

"So you knew it was wrong, but you went along with it anyway," she said.

Roland nodded. "I can't blame Al or anyone else. The fault was mine."

She felt her cheeks grow warm. "So you thought you might as well join in the fun and kiss Emma Mae?"

"Ne." Roland shook his head. "It wasn't like that. We were playing a game—shucking corn to see who was fastest. Emma Mae got the red ear of corn, and the other kids started shouting, 'Forfeit! Forfeit!'"

Johanna gritted her teeth.

"Al yelled for Emma Mae to kiss a guy for her forfeit, and everybody started clapping and stamping their feet. She picked me, and—"

"You didn't say no."

Roland shook his head. "I didn't say no."

Johanna turned her head away, but she couldn't

keep the familiar ache from rising in her chest. It still hurt, after all this time.

"Emma Mae…wasn't a pretty girl. She was plain, really plain, with big teeth, and all I could think was that if I turned her down, everybody would laugh at her."

"You didn't care that it would hurt me."

He exhaled softly. "None of us thought the Pennsylvania State Police would bust into the barn with searchlights, bullhorns and half the church elders in Lancaster. Everyone went crazy. Kids were running in all directions, trying to get out of there. One of the guys threw his beer, and it splashed all over me. That's why the police thought I'd been drinking. Because I smelled like beer."

Johanna's eyes narrowed. "Go on."

"We were taken into the police station for alcohol breathalyzer tests."

"And you were unlucky enough to have some newspaper reporter take your picture as you were being loaded into the police van? The picture we all saw in the Englisher newspaper."

"*Ya,* I was," he said.

She considered his explanation. Roland had never lied to her. If he said that he hadn't intended to kiss Emma Mae, she had to take him at his word. But… She inhaled deeply, feeling almost dizzy. Was that really all that had happened? Had

she really changed the outcome of her whole life…
of *their* lives, for something so small?

"I passed the test, Johanna," Roland said. "The
machine didn't register any alcohol on my breath.
I *looked* guilty, but it proved that I was innocent,
and they didn't press charges against me. I was
never arrested for underage drinking."

Johanna remembered, with a sick feeling, that
the opinions in the Amish community had been
harsh after the incident. Sermons had been preached
against evil and worldly behavior. The bishop
had named Roland Byler as one of those who had
shamed the faith, his parents and community.
Even *Dat,* who rarely lost his temper, had been
furious with what Roland had done.

"Johanna?"

"I don't know what to say, Roland."

"I'm not the stupid boy I was then. That one
mistake cost me everything. You know that I repented and joined the church. Since then, I've tried
to live our faith as best I can."

"So this is all my fault?"

"Doesn't the Bible teach us to forgive? If I
wronged you—and I did—haven't I made up for
it? It's time for you to forgive me. Truly forgive
me. It's the only way we can go on from here."

She pressed her fingertips to her forehead.
"Why didn't you come to me after it happened,

Roland? I loved you then. It would have been so much easier if you—"

"But I *did* come," he insisted. "Don't you remember? As soon as I got home from Lancaster. I went to your house to explain, but Jonas turned me away."

"Dat?" She stared down at him in disbelief. *"Dat* kept you from speaking to me?"

"Ya. He said I was not the kind of man he wanted as a husband to you and a father to your children. He told me not to set foot on his land again."

She shook her head slowly. "He wouldn't have done that."

"I asked him if you felt the same way, and he said you did. He said I had nothing to say that you wanted to hear—that we were finished."

"I didn't know," she murmured, looking down, then back at him. "And you believed him? That I wouldn't want to talk face-to-face? Does that sound like me?"

He shrugged his broad shoulders. "Again, I was young. And embarrassed and feeling so guilty. I thought of Jonas as more than a friend, almost as a second father. Why wouldn't I have believed him?"

"So you went away."

"Ya. I left Delaware the following day, spent the summer harvesting grain in Kansas and Nebraska. And when I finally came home, Mary

told me that you were promised to Wilmer Detweiler, and that you seemed happy. I didn't want to hurt you again...I thought it was too late for us."

The tears that had threatened were gone, replaced with an emptiness. Could *Dat* really have sent him away and never told her? She didn't want to believe it, but Roland had never lied to her... and *Dat* wasn't here to ask.

"You need to give me time to think," she said as she reached for the reins again. "This is a lot to think about."

This time, he placed the reins in her hands. "You can go, but you can't keep running from the truth. It's not what I did at that frolic that you've held against me all these years. It's that I embarrassed you. It's your pride that has kept us apart, Johanna. And it's your pride that keeps you from admitting that you still love me."

Anger flared in her chest and she lifted the reins. His words were so hurtful. "That's the way you feel?"

"It is."

"Then I'll take that as a refusal of my proposal. You can consider our courtship officially ended," she said, looking straight ahead. "You were right. It's too late for us, Roland. If I am so stubborn and full of pride, I'm not the woman you want as a wife."

* * *

All the way home from the horse farm, Johanna tried to hold herself together. She didn't dare shed a single tear; she had to pick up Katy from Fannie and Roman's, and if she allowed herself to weaken, she'd fall apart. Having Fannie and her children or Katy see her cry wasn't something she wanted to do.

At Fannie's, Katy had come running, full of chatter about her visit and spilling over with questions about her aunt Ruth's new baby boys. Fannie and her girls had been just as excited, and Johanna had been forced to pretend a joyfulness she didn't feel at the moment. Not that she wasn't thrilled for Ruth and Eli, or that she didn't welcome the twins wholeheartedly. But the confrontation she'd had with Roland had her shaking inside.

When she and Katy had finally taken their leave of Fannie and driven home, Johanna had hoped to find a quiet corner where she could think. But there seemed to be none. Although Eli had taken Ruth and the boys home to sleep in their own beds, *Mam's* place was still teeming with family.

Rebecca had offered to keep Anna's children while she went to make supper for the new parents, and—much to Katy's delight—the three girls were running in and out of the house in a spirited game of tag, cheered on by Susanna. Irwin, Rudy, Peter and two of Irwin's cousins were playing ball in the pasture beside the barn. Aunt Jezzy and Nip Hilty were sitting on the front porch, snapping string beans. Johanna's hope that she could escape to solitude in the garden was dashed by Susanna's declaration that *Mam* and Miriam were in the garden setting out a row of zucchini plants.

The kitchen was no better. Aunt Martha and *Grossmama* were trying to teach Lydia Beachy a fancy stitch they were using to knit sweaters for Ruth's babies, and Dorcas was putting together a huge pan of blueberry crisp. As Katy scrambled to catch up with Anna's Lori Ann, Mae and Naomi, Rebecca came out of the pantry with a bucket and mop. She'd just finished scrubbing the floor and was about to do the same in the downstairs bathroom and front parlor.

Johanna tried to make small talk with her aunt and cousin, agreeing that, yes, Ruth's twins looked like Yoders, and no, her labor hadn't been long, all the while edging her way toward the far doorway. Johanna loved her family and she was used to having a lot of people around her. But she didn't want to look foolish by bursting into tears and she certainly didn't want to have to explain to Aunt Martha the reason for such outlandish behavior.

Aunt Martha's pointed questions about whether *Mam* had planted an unusual amount of celery this year, and if Johanna thought there might be any more surprise announcements at the next church meeting, was the final straw. "I have to go!" Johanna said and fled the kitchen.

By the time she reached the bottom of the steps, all Johanna's self-control was gone and she was sobbing with great noisy gasps. Almost blindly she raced up the steps, down the second-floor hallway and into her bedroom. She slammed the door behind her and flung herself across her neatly made bed.

Tears came in floods. She buried her face in her Star of Bethlehem quilt and wept until she could hardly catch her breath. She was still crying when a persistent rapping at the door broke through her misery.

"Go away," she said. "Leave me alone."

"Johanna? Are you all right?" It was Rebecca's voice.

"Please," she said. "I just want to…be…" Another sob. "Alone."

The door hinges squeaked, and Johanna heard footsteps on the pine floorboards. "What's wrong?" The mattress gave as Rebecca sank down on the bed beside her. She handed her the tissue box from the table beside the bed. "Tell me what's going on."

"Roland," Johanna rasped.

"Ah."

"We… He… I went to…"

Rebecca handed her a tissue. "Blow your nose," she ordered. "Did you and Roland argue?"

"Ya...ne..." Johanna sat up, blew her nose and used a clean tissue to wipe her eyes. She sniffed. "I went to find him, to tell him that we should stop with the courting and..." Somehow, although she hadn't meant to, everything spilled out. And Rebecca, in her quiet, comforting way, sat and listened patiently to her story.

"And the worst part was, he...he called me prideful," Johanna said.

Rebecca sighed. "And you denied it?"

Johanna nodded. "He said I haven't been able to forgive him for embarrassing me." She took a shuddering breath. "He said that when he came back from Lancaster, he came here to try to explain to me what had happened, but *Dat* sent him away."

"Which *Dat* did." Rebecca pushed a damp lock of hair off Johanna's forehead and searched her gaze. "But you didn't know?"

"I didn't know," Johanna whispered.

"Oh, dear." Rebecca sighed. "I thought you knew. Everyone in the family did. *Mam* was not happy with *Dat,* and they had words over it."

Johanna's looked at her sister in astonishment. "How do you know?"

Rebecca shrugged. "I heard them. I was eating grapes on the far side of the arbor when *Mam* and *Dat* came into the backyard." A hint of mischief danced in her eyes. "I did what every young girl does when she hears adults quarreling. I listened."

Johanna closed her eyes for a moment. "This changes everything."

Rebecca shook her head. "No, it doesn't. What Roland did or didn't do at that frolic, what *Dat* said or didn't say, doesn't matter as much as what you're doing right now. Roland is right. You wouldn't forgive him, because he'd hurt your pride. I don't say this to hurt you, sister, but I always thought you married Wilmer to spite Roland. I thought you did it to show everyone that you could get a husband—a more Godly man than Roland Byler."

"Everyone always tells me that I'm stubborn, but it's not my greatest fault," Johanna mused aloud. "It's pride. How could I be so foolish?" She buried her face in her hands.

Rebecca rubbed her back. "I think maybe it's fear, too."

"Fear?" Johanna dabbed a tissue under her nose.

"You're afraid of loving him. Because you do."

"Because I do love him," Johanna whispered. The thought came to her with another flood of emotions. Of course she loved him. She'd always loved him. All these years. "I've ruined everything," she whispered to her sister.

"Nonsense. There's nothing you've said or done that can't be fixed if you're truly sorry."

More hot tears slipped down Johanna's cheeks.

"You don't understand. I broke off our…our court-ship. I knew what Roland said was true, but I wouldn't admit it. I told him I didn't want him for a husband."

"But do you?"

She looked up at Rebecca. "I do," she admitted. "I want to marry him because it's the right thing to do…but also because I love him."

"So go to him and tell him. If Roland truly loves you, and he does, he'll forgive you. You two can go back to courting and marry and make each other miserable for the rest of your lives."

Johanna pulled away from her sister. "Rebecca!"

"Just teasing you. Go on. Go to him." She chuckled. "But don't go until you've washed your face and made yourself pretty. You can't ask him to marry you with a red nose and swollen eyes and hair sticking out all over like a haystack. That's not how you persuade a man to do what you want him to do."

"Rebecca Yoder," Johanna exclaimed in aston-ishment, dabbing at her eyes with another tissue. "What would a modest *maedle* know about per-suading men?"

Rebecca's chuckle became a merry giggle. "Some things, sister, a girl is just born knowing."

Chapter Seventeen

Deciding to go back to Roland and admit that she was wrong was easier said than done. First, there was the question as to whether or not he was still too angry to listen to reason. Second, there was the possibility that he would refuse her apology and tell her that marrying a prideful woman like her was the furthest thing from his mind. And third, maybe most important, was the when and how she should make her case to Roland. How was she going to make him believe that she truly did love him with all her heart? That what Rebecca said was true. That it was also fear that had made her behave the way she had.

As always, once she'd made up her mind, Johanna was eager to carry out her mission. But getting away from the house at suppertime was nearly impossible. There was the family to feed, the children to look after and a stream of visitors to welcome and share the good news about Ruth and Eli's babies. And as the eldest unmarried daughter, a good portion of the work fell to her.

Had she simply gone to *Mam* and told her how important it was for her to speak with Roland this evening, her mother would have insisted that she go at once. But *Mam* was rushing about, sixteen to a dozen. Rebecca's and Susanna's hands were busy looking after the Yoder children and those of their guests, keeping them from falling out of the hayloft, or climbing into the pigpen to cuddle one of the piglets that had been born two days earlier.

Of course, there were the usual evening chores that had to be done on even an ordinary summer day. Cows had to be fed and milked, horses turned into their stalls and given measures of grain. Turkeys had to be driven and penned for the night against the threat of stray dogs and foxes, and sheep had to be counted and driven into their fold.

With Irwin a part of the household, the care of the animals should have fallen to him, but so far he had proved more trouble than he was worth as a help around the farm. Susanna had more sense when it came to locking gates behind her, remembering to check to see if water troughs were filled, and knowing that cows could kick over milk buckets. It wasn't enough for *Mam* or Johanna to ask Irwin if the animals had been properly seen to. They had to ask about each task specifically.

Otherwise, one cow might be forgotten, or the first person in the barn for morning milking might discover a lid off the feed barrel and a mouse feast in progress. Tonight, *Mam* was too busy receiving neighbors, so the task of managing Irwin fell to Johanna.

Once supper was cleared away and the animals content, Johanna might have slipped away, except for the arrival of Bishop Atlee and his wife with chicken potpies, a pound cake and a baked ham for Ruth and Eli.

"We'd not think of bothering them tonight," the bishop said, "or you. I'm sure everyone in Kent County has stopped by to offer their good wishes and prayers for your daughter and her sons, but I know one of your girls won't mind just running these things over. No need for Ruth to trouble herself by cooking."

"No need," *Mam* had echoed with hearty smile. And no need for her to make less of the bishop's wife's contributions by telling either of them that everyone who'd come by today had brought food for the young household.

Buns and streusels, pies and tins of cookies shared the pantry table and shelves with jars of pickles, chow-chow, hard-boiled eggs pickled in beet juice, potato salad, macaroni salad, spiced peaches, relish and blackberry jam. There was a rice pudding sprinkled with nutmeg, a pan of freshly made scrapple, three bowls of coleslaw, a jellied veal loaf, a roasted duck, a German noodle ring and at least one kettle of clam chowder and a second of split-pea soup.

Whether the new twins were to consume all this food or Eli and the new mother, Johanna wasn't sure. But one thing was for certain: the Yoders, the Masts, and Charley and Miriam would eat well for the next week, without any of the women having to cook. And every giver would be thanked as sincerely as if they were the only ones who'd been so thoughtful as to think of providing a meal for Ruth and Eli's table.

As Bishop Atlee's buggy rolled out of the yard, Rebecca pulled Johanna aside. "Why haven't you gone to Roland's yet?" she demanded. "Have you lost your nerve?" She frowned. "If you wait until tomorrow, you'll just make the situation worse."

"The children…"

"Grace and I will put Katy and Jonah to bed. Go."

Johanna glanced at her mother, who was standing on the back porch watching them intently. "What does she know?" Johanna whispered to her sister. "You didn't tell her anything I told you, did you?"

"*Ne.* Shall I tell Irwin to hitch up Blackie?"

"If I take the buggy, *Mam* will ask why and

I'll have to explain. I'll just walk over. It's not that far."

"Don't chicken out on me," Rebecca warned.

"What do you two have your heads together about?" Grace called from the porch, where she'd joined *Mam*. "I'm just going over to Ruth's to take this clam chowder. There's no more room in the refrigerator. If one of you comes with me, you can carry a bowl of sliced peaches."

Rebecca looked at Johanna.

"I'll go," Johanna called. And then to Rebecca, she whispered, "It's hardly any farther from Ruth's to Roland's. I'll just stay a minute, and that way *Mam* won't—"

"Know what you're up to," Rebecca finished. "Okay, but hurry, or your potential betrothed will be asleep before you tell him the good news."

As the two walked to Ruth's, Johanna filled Grace in on what had happened earlier in the day between her and Roland. "I don't know how I could have been so blind," she confessed as they crossed the field with their heavy containers of food. "Our church teaches us that pride is wrong, but all I could see was what Roland had done to me."

"It'll all work out," Grace said. "I know he's crazy about you."

Miriam pushed open the back door. "Come on

in," she called to her sisters. "Adam is awake. Wait until you see those gorgeous eyes."

Johanna and Grace followed her into the house, and soon they were admiring the twins, chatting with a sleepy Ruth and inquiring as to how she felt. For a few minutes, Johanna was caught up in the excitement of the babies and her sister's happiness.

Just ten more minutes. Roland will still be up. It won't hurt to stay here with Ruth and my sisters a little while longer. It will be easier to talk to Roland if J.J.'s in bed when I get there. She'd almost convinced herself that she was worried for nothing, that the explanation and Roland's forgiveness would come easily, when Charley burst in with news.

"Roland's got company," Charley announced to the room. "And it means trouble." He fixed his gaze on Johanna.

"What are you talking about?" Miriam balanced Luke against her shoulder and patted his back. "What trouble?"

Charley shoved his hands into his pockets. "I just came from there."

"And?" Ruth asked. "You know you're going to explode if you don't tell us."

"Well, it's not like I haven't said this might happen," Charley went on, obviously pleased to be the center of attention. "You know that Lancaster girl, the one who works at the cheese shop at Spence's Market? The one who's had her eye on Roland?"

"She's at his house?" Grace asked. "The girl?"

"Not the girl," Charley answered. "Her father and two of her uncles, come all the way from Lancaster. They hired a driver and—"

"We don't care how they got here." Miriam passed the baby to Ruth. "What are they doing here? What do they want with Roland?"

"From what the driver said, her father's eager to find her a husband. She's got two younger sisters who've had offers, but can't marry until she does. And apparently, she's picky."

"But what does that have to do with Roland?" Johanna asked, all too certain that she already knew the answer.

"The driver said the girl has set her *Kapp* for Roland. The father has already asked a lot of questions about Roland, and now they've come to look him over. The driver says they want to offer the girl to him as a wife—one that comes with one hundred acres of Lancaster farmland, a house and a stone barn as a dowry."

Eli let out a low whistle. "A hundred-acre farm. In Lancaster. Land up there is worth a fortune. It will be hard for Roland to pass up." He rolled his eyes innocently toward the ceiling. "Especially since things haven't worked out here for him. He might decide moving to Pennsylvania would be in his best interest."

"What do you mean they haven't *worked out?*" Ruth asked. "He's been courting Johanna. Who would throw Johanna over for a cheese girl and a stone barn in the middle of a cow pasture?"

"There's a herd of cows that comes with the pasture," Charley teased. "The driver says—"

Miriam silenced him with a look.

Grace turned to Johanna. "I suppose it's too late for you to make a counteroffer—to keep him from accepting these Lancaster people."

"If it was me," Miriam said, "I wouldn't have let Charley go without putting up a fight."

A smile teased at the corners of Grace's mouth. "I thought you Amish were against fighting."

"There's fighting and then there's fighting," Johanna answered softly. "And as *Dat* always said, it's never too late to pray for rain until the barn has already burned down."

Grace got out of the car and gave Johanna a hug. "It's really dark. Are you sure you don't want a flashlight? I've got one in the glove box. Or I could drive you up to the house."

"Ne," Johanna answered. "I can see well enough to walk up the lane. And I'd rather no one saw me coming."

"Good luck." Grace gave her a kiss on the cheek.

"*Ya.* I think I'll need it." Johanna turned away from the vehicle and started up the drive at a quick pace. She didn't know what she was going to do or say when she got to the house, but she couldn't stop now. If she hesitated, she might lose her nerve.

Roland's yard was dark. A soft glow from the kitchen and parlor propane lamps spilled through the open windows. Around her, lightning bugs flashed, and frogs and crickets chirped the melody of a muggy summer night.

The day that had begun so sunny had turned damp and there was the oppressive feel of approaching rain. In the distance, Johanna could hear the rumble of thunder. It was that way in Delaware. As the old folks were fond of saying, "If you don't like the weather, wait half an hour and it will change." She was glad she hadn't brought the buggy. She wasn't afraid of a storm, but Blackie was. Better to depend on her own two feet.

Feet that were now carrying her closer and closer to Roland and a situation that might be beyond her ability to make right. She was scared, scared to the bone. Her heart was racing, her thoughts were all in a jumble, and her stomach made her wish she hadn't eaten that cup of chowder earlier. What would she do if she walked into Roland's kitchen and threw up all over his shoes? That would be embarrassing, but not as devastating as finding out that Roland and the cheese girl's father had already come to an agreement, shaken hands on the deal and set a date for marriage banns to be read.

She had been a fool. She'd been stubborn, prideful and fearful, and she'd let the man the Lord had sent her slip through her fingers. How could she have been so concerned with a silly incident that had happened years ago? How could she have failed to see that she was throwing away her future happiness and security out of her own weaknesses? Not only was she ruining the chances of a happy marriage, she was spoiling everything for three innocent children.

Mam had told her; Ruth, Rebecca, Anna, Miriam and Grace had told her. Even Susanna had seemed to understand that Roland and J.J. were already part of the family.

"Please, God," Johanna prayed under her breath. "I know I don't deserve a second chance, but Katy and Jonah and J.J. do. Roland does. And if you please help me out of this jam, I promise I'll never…"

She stopped and exhaled softly, then sucked in lungs full of the humid air. "I'll try harder," she promised. "I'll do what I can to curb my pride and stubbornness. I promise I'll do everything I can to be the best wife any man could ever want."

She was nearing the house now. The black

shadows of lilac bushes loomed on either side of the drive. Through the open windows, she heard Roland's sister Mary and the answering rumble of a man's voice. She listened for Roland, but didn't hear him. Then came a second voice, injecting something she couldn't make out. He spoke in Pennsylvania *Deutch,* his distinctly Lancaster accent giving a different lilt to his comment.

Johanna was tempted to creep close to the window to find out what was happening, if what Charley had said was true, but rejected that as too petty. No, she would have to confront her rivals head-on. With her father dead and no uncle she could count on to speak for her, she was on her own.

She moved on quiet feet, through the gloom, toward the back door. Blood pounded in her ears. Her fingers and toes felt numb. As the first drops of rain splattered on her face, she felt as if were wading through thick mud. "Just a few more steps," she muttered.

Abruptly, she slammed into something in the darkness. Not something—someone. A cry of fright rose from her throat to be cut off by the sensation of arms wrapping around her and strong fingers clapping over her mouth.

"Johanna," Roland whispered urgently. "Don't be scared. It's just me."

"Roland?" she mumbled.

He removed his hand. "Shh," he repeated. "They'll hear you."

Her heart settled back into her chest, but she was so light-headed that she swayed in his arms, nearly losing her balance. Roland's strong arms held her as a shimmering wave of rain enveloped them both.

"Come on," he urged. "We'll get soaked out here." He caught her hand and dashed away from the house back toward the barn. Not knowing what else to do, she ran with him.

When the barn loomed above, Roland flung open the door and pulled her inside. Instantly, she was enveloped in the warm, sweet smells of fresh-cut hay, molasses, oats and horses. "What are you doing out there in the dark?" she demanded.

"That was close," he said. "What are *you* doing here? I didn't know what was coming out of the dark. You scared me half—"

"*I* scared *you?* How do you think…" Suddenly, it struck her as funny. Roland's visitors were inside, and he was outside in the bushes. A snort of amusement bubbled up from the pit of her belly in her throat. "You were hiding from them," she declared.

"No, I wasn't."

"Yes, you were." The snort became a chuckle and then a peal of laughter. "Roland Byler, you are such a fibber."

"Shh, they'll hear you." He pulled her deeper into the familiar sanctuary of the barn. "What was I supposed to say to them?"

"'Hello. How can I help you?' That might be a start," she whispered with a giggle. He was still holding her hand, but she was no longer his captive…more his partner in crime. "If you didn't speak to them, how did you know who they were and why they've come?"

"Oh, I know why they're here. They got here first, but I met their driver at the end of the lane. Mary was still—" He broke off. "What were you doing hiding in my bushes?"

"I had to come. Charley told me they were here."

"My brother couldn't keep a secret if his crop depended on it. I didn't want you to know—"

"What?" She felt a little pang of fear. Maybe she *was* too late. "I was supposed to learn that you were marrying your Lancaster cheese peddler when the bishop cried your banns at next service?"

He pulled her into the circle of his arms, and she knew in her heart of hearts that she wasn't too late. She inhaled deeply of the damp, clean, male scent of him. *Safe. I feel safe here. This is where I belong.*

"Don't be *lecherich,* Johanna," Roland said. "How could I have two wives? I still intend to marry you, once you realize that I'm right, and that you love me, and that it was your stubborn pride—"

"That kept us apart," she finished. "And my fear…my fear of loving you. Of knowing how much I've loved you all along." He brushed his fingertips across her cheek and joy blossomed inside her. "So you weren't going to accept the offer of a rich farm and a stone barn full of cows? Pretty *dumm* to take a sharp-tongued widow with only a few scraggly sheep and—"

"She has a stone barn and cows?" he interrupted.

She dug her fingers into his side and he laughed.

"Bees," he said. "You have lots of bees."

"And turkeys."

Roland lowered his head, the teasing gone from his voice. "I know you, Johanna. I knew when you left the horse farm that it was only a matter of time before you thought it through and realized—"

"That I love you," she finished, realizing she could hold nothing back from Roland. Not ever again.

"Almost as much as I love you."

His lips brushed hers in a tender kiss that sent all her fears flying into the night. For a long moment, she savored the feel of his mouth and the warmth of his arms before she stepped away. "Best that waits awhile longer," she whispered breath-lessly. "Or…"

"Or we will both be on our knees in front of the congregation," he agreed.

For another moment or two, they remained bod-ies apart, but fingers still laced together. Johanna listened to the rain on the roof, the movement of the horses in their stalls, and the sound of Roland's breathing. "What now?" she asked him.

"Now I go in and thank our visitors for their kind offer," he said.

"That they haven't made yet. And…" She waited, certain he already knew what he would say that would make everything right.

"And I tell them that I'm honored that they'd think of me, but I've already spoken to my preacher about calling the banns for my wedding to the widow Johanna Detweiler."

"You would lie to them?"

This time it was Roland who laughed. "Johanna, my love. I've known you too long and faced your temper too many times. It burns fierce and hot, but in the end, your sense of fairness wins out. I knew that, sooner or later, you would come to tell me you were sorry and loved me more than bread and honey."

"You did not!" she accused, barely able to con-tain another burst of laughter.

"Ah, but I did. Ask him. John and I stopped by

the bishop's house on the way home. After that, it was just a matter of waiting for you to come to your senses. The visitors from Lancaster nearly upset all my plans. What if you hadn't given in and come tonight? How could I have told them that I was already betrothed before I was?"

"But you could tell Bishop Atlee we were?"

"*Ne.* I simply asked him to cry the banns. I never said you had agreed to marry me."

"And if I'd said no?"

"But you said yes, didn't you? You and I will take our vows as soon as is decent, our children will have a mother and a father again, and the cheese seller's daughter will have to seek out another bridegroom."

And that was exactly the way it all happened....

274

Epilogue

 ❧

Nine Months Later...

It was a wet March Saturday, too mild for a last blast of winter and too blustery for the coming spring. For two days, heavy rain had pelted the roofs and roads and fields of Seven Poplars, driven the livestock inside to seek shelter and sent Vs of wild geese flying north overhead, honking their plaintive cries.

The rain didn't trouble the Amish community, as a whole. The farmers and their wives welcomed the downpour because it filled their wells and soaked the newly plowed fields. Soon, seeds would go into the fertile earth, and the moisture would ensure lush crops of grain, vegetables and hay. The children, however, cooped up inside for days, yearned to have the chance to burn up their energy. They wanted to shout without being told to lower their voices, play ball, climb trees and cast the first baited hooks and bobbers into ponds.

But the rain continued to fall, and heavy, gray clouds offered no hint of sunshine and no chance to enjoy what should have been a fun-filled Saturday, after a week of school. Or so Jonah and J.J. thought.

They didn't know what their parents were up to. Enlisting Katy as a coconspirator, Johanna and Roland had made a plan for a great adventure. First, J.J. and Jonah were both blindfolded and led to the family buggy. Then, they were driven around—where, they didn't know, much to a giggling Katy's delight. The only hint as to what the adventure might be was the tantalizing smell of gingerbread, barbecued chicken, baked beans and *knabru*s that drifted from the back of the carriage.

"Where are we going?" J.J. asked for the tenth time.

Johanna chuckled. "We can't tell you. It's a surprise."

"It's a pic—" Katy squealed, covering her mouth with her hands. "A surprise," she repeated.

"But when will we get there?" Jonah demanded. "We've been driving for hours."

Roland laughed. "Hardly, but…" He reined in his roan and the buggy came to a stop. "We're almost there."

"Hurray!" both boys cried in unison.

"Hurray!" Katy shouted and then dissolved into giggles again.

Johanna waited until Roland had opened the double doors wide and then guided the horse and buggy inside the barn. "Don't take your blindfolds off yet," she warned. "You'll spoil the surprise." She knotted the leathers around the dashboard rail, climbed down and helped Katy out of the carriage.

Roland closed the doors behind them and lifted first Jonah and then J.J. down from the vehicle. "It *is* a picnic," he declared, "but a special one."

"How can you have a picnic in the rain?" J.J. asked, practically vibrating with excitement.

"Wait and see." Johanna took J.J.'s hand and led him to the base of the ladder that led to the hayloft, while Roland did the same for Jonah. "Now, take off your blindfolds."

Both whipped the bandanas off their faces.

"Aw, it's just our barn," Jonah said, turning around.

"*Ya,* just our barn," J.J. echoed, dejectedly.

"*Ne.*" Johanna chuckled. "That's what *you* think. It's our special picnic spot where no other boy in Seven Poplars has ever picnicked before."

"Up the ladder," Roland ordered as he removed the heavy baskets from the back of the buggy.

Soon Johanna and Katy, J.J., Jonah and Roland were all standing on the floor of the hayloft. This winter, this part of the loft had been used to store straw, and earlier today, Johanna had covered some of the bales with clean white sheets to make a table. There were plates and mugs and napkins, and standing beside the straw table was a shiny new bucket with thermoses of hot chocolate for everyone.

"Wunderbar!" Katy exclaimed. "A kitchen in the hayloft!"

"Who's hungry?" Johanna asked. In moments, Roland had brought up the picnic baskets from the buggy, and the bowls and pans of food were on the table. The family gathered around to hold hands and bow their heads for the moment of silent grace that signaled the beginning of every meal.

Katy's enthusiasm was catching, and soon the boys were having as much fun as she was. Everyone laughed and talked and ate until they were stuffed, and when the two boys begged for one last gingerbread man, Johanna couldn't help but allow them the additional treat. Afterward, she cleared away the dishes, tucked the containers back into the picnic baskets and Roland drew a deck of Dutch Blitz cards out of his pocket.

"Games!" J.J. cried. He loved games, especially Old Maid and Go Fish and checkers. Katy was just learning the rules, but J.J. was especially brotherly to her, helping her with her choices and cheering on her moves.

The family card game was followed by a story

about a fishing trip that Roland had taken with their *Grossdaddi* Yoder, one that the boys loved because it always ended with *Mam* catching more fish than *Dat*.

After the last chuckle had faded, Johanna brought out the big children's Bible storybook that her mother had given her and read the story of Noah and the Flood. The rain beating against the cedar roof shingles made a perfect background for the old and familiar tale. They all listened in silence to Johanna's words and sighed with contentment at the end when Noah opened the doors of the Ark and the people saw green.

"This is the best picnic ever!" Jonah pronounced.

"The best," J.J. agreed.

Katy yawned and nodded her approval.

"Just one more thing," Johanna said, glancing at Roland. He nodded, rose and climbed back down the ladder.

After a few minutes, he returned to the barn and called up. "You children might want to come down. There's something here that I think belongs to you."

"What?" Jonah asked.

All three small heads leaned over the opening to the ladder.

"You'll have to come down. Katy first."

One by one, the children descended the ladder. Johanna watched from the hayloft as Roland reached into a feed barrel and lifted out a wriggling bundle of black-and-white fur. Two black eyes peered out from under a fringe of hair, and a small, pink, puppy tongue licked at Katy's cheek.

"Es hundli!" she squealed. "Is it ours? To keep?"

"If you love him and care for him," Johanna called down. "He's a Bernese Mountain Dog, and he'll get a lot bigger."

After delivering a few instructions about how to handle the puppy, Roland left the children below and climbed back up the ladder to join Johanna. "That should keep them busy for a while," he said.

Johanna leaned close and kissed his cheek. "You are the best father any child could want," she said. "You spoil them."

"I hope not." He enfolded her hand in his and squeezed it gently. "I hope I raise them with love and care, so that they will grow to be good and faithful members of our church and community."

"I am proud of you."

His eyes lit with mischief. "Pride from the mother of my children? I thought you had put that all behind you when we took our vows."

She chuckled. "I am a work in progress, Roland Byler, and don't you forget it."

"But a good mother," he said, becoming serious, "and a good wife."

"I try. Every day, I open my eyes and thank God

for you and our family, and I promise myself to work at being worthy of His blessings."

"You make me happy," he said, glancing deeper into the loft, then back at her. "But there's something…"

"*Ya?* What is it, Roland?"

"I've always wanted to take a pretty *frau* into the hayloft and kiss her."

"Roland Byler, and you a married man," she teased, but she picked up a clean sheet and spread it over a pile of loose straw. "So what's keeping you from it?"

He put his arm around her and they sank into the soft and fragrant bed. For a long time, they lay together, her head on his shoulder, not speaking, listening to the sweet sounds of their children's voices and the rain on the roof before she spoke. "Is this what you wanted?"

"*Ya.*" He sighed with contentment and kissed her cheek. "Exactly what I dreamed about. You, Johanna, no other, just you beside me."

"Not just me," she corrected. "Not exactly. There is another."

Puzzled, he glanced into her face. "Another?"

She laughed softly. "For an observant man, there is much you don't see, husband."

"What are you talking about?"

"Something I have wanted for a long time."

"What is it, Johanna? I'll give you whatever you wish, if I can…if I can afford it."

She lay back against him and snuggled close. "This, I think we can afford. I want you to place an order from Eli, at the chair shop."

"You want a chair?"

Johanna chuckled. "*Ne,* my love, not a chair. A cradle."

He sat bolt upright and stared at her. "A cradle? You mean you… We?"

She laughed again, raised her face and kissed him full on the mouth. "Is it so surprising that the Lord who could save Noah and all his people from the flood can't provide us with one small baby?" And then a doubt threw a shadow over her excitement. "You are happy, aren't you? To be a father again?"

But Roland didn't need to answer because the look in his eyes told her all she needed to know. And the tears that spilled down her cheeks were ones of pure joy.

* * * * *

Dear Reader,

Hello! It's so good to see you. I'm always happy to welcome old friends back to Seven Poplars and so pleased to meet new readers, as well. The Amish countryside is so beautiful at this time of the year. Did you pass any horse and buggies on your way here? Please, sit down. I've just taken butter cookies out of the oven, and I was about to make some lemonade. It would be so nice if you'd join me.

If you have questions about my Old Order Amish neighbors, I'd be happy to answer them. Despite the different style of clothing and sense of tradition, they aren't so different from you. Family, faith and community come first. They're a strong, joyful people who seek love, companionship and a sense of self-worth as much as any of us. Don't make the mistake of believing that Amish women are meek or subservient to men. According to their rules, everyone is equal under heaven. The Amish try every day to live according to God's word, and they take to heart our Lord's admonition to love one another.

Do you believe in second chances? Johanna and Roland were sweethearts as young adults, but a bad decision and misunderstanding tore them apart. Now, Amish custom urges them both to marry again, but Johanna wonders if she believes in romantic love anymore. To complicate matters, both are already parents, and they face the problems of trying to blend two families. If you've followed the Hannah's Daughters series, you know that Johanna has a mind of her own. Hopefully, Roland is a match for her.

What's next? I'll share a secret. I've always loved the story of Beauty and the Beast. A fairy-tale romance plays out in Seven Poplars when Rebecca sets her *Kapp* for the mysterious new preacher. Do come back and share her story with me.

Wishing you peace and joy,
Your friend,
Emma Miller

Questions for Discussion

1. Why do you think Johanna was so reluctant to accept Roland's offer to court her? Was it because she didn't like him, or was she happy remaining unmarried?

2. What effect did Johanna's troubled life with Wilmer have on her view of marriage? Do you believe she was abused? Have you known a woman who has been abused? How did she handle the situation?

3. Do you believe that Johanna blamed herself for her husband's mental illness and the taking of his own life? Did she blame God? Did you feel that her personal faith remained strong?

4. What good things did Johanna bring from her first marriage? Do you think she was a good mother? How important do you think it is for children to be raised with a strong male role figure in their lives?

5. Johanna is Hannah's oldest daughter. Does being the oldest child in a family change the way that an individual deals with life's problems? Do you think a single child or the oldest of siblings feels more responsibility than

a middle child or the youngest? Did Johanna set a good example for her younger sisters?

6. Amish tradition dictates that a young woman who is widowed remarry, and almost all widows do so. Do you think that Johanna questions her choice because her mother hasn't remarried? Does Aunt Jezzy's choice make a difference?

7. The Amish family structure is very traditional. Do you think it would be difficult for a woman like Johanna to submit to the authority of a husband as her church teaches? Would it be for you personally?

8. The Amish culture centers around family and church community. To be Old Order Amish, an individual must submit to the *Ordnung,* or rule of the church. In your opinion, is Johanna rebelling against the rule by delaying marriage? Do you believe that she ever thought of leaving the Amish faith as one of her sisters did?

9. Was it obvious to you as a reader that Roland is the right man for Johanna? Do you think he was changed by the death of his wife? Is he a good father? Do you think he'll make a good father for Katy and Jonah?

10. What do you believe is Johanna's biggest challenge in the story? Do you believe that she and Roland will be able to put the past behind them and create a strong, loving family? Do you believe that her own childhood, coming from a caring family and seeing her parents' marriage work, increases the chances of her own success?

LARGER-PRINT BOOKS!

GET 2 FREE
LARGER-PRINT NOVELS
PLUS 2 FREE
MYSTERY GIFTS

Love Inspired

Larger-print novels are now available...

YES! Please send me 2 FREE LARGER-PRINT Love Inspired® novels and my 2 FREE mystery gifts (gifts are worth about $10). After receiving them, if I don't wish to receive any more books, I can return the shipping statement marked "cancel." If I don't cancel, I will receive 6 brand-new novels every month and be billed just $5.24 per book in the U.S. or $5.74 per book in Canada. That's a savings of at least 23% off the cover price. It's quite a bargain! Shipping and handling is just 50¢ per book in the U.S. and 75¢ per book in Canada.* I understand that accepting the 2 free books and gifts places me under no obligation to buy anything. I can always return a shipment and cancel at any time. Even if I never buy another book, the two free books and gifts are mine to keep forever.

122/322 IDN F49Y

Name	(PLEASE PRINT)	

Address		Apt. #

City	State/Prov.	Zip/Postal Code

Signature (if under 18, a parent or guardian must sign)

Mail to the Harlequin® Reader Service:
IN U.S.A.: P.O. Box 1867, Buffalo, NY 14240-1867
IN CANADA: P.O. Box 609, Fort Erie, Ontario L2A 5X3

**Are you a current subscriber to Love Inspired books
and want to receive the larger-print edition?
Call 1-800-873-8635 or visit www.ReaderService.com.**

* Terms and prices subject to change without notice. Prices do not include applicable taxes. Sales tax applicable in N.Y. Canadian residents will be charged applicable taxes. Offer not valid in Quebec. This offer is limited to one order per household. Not valid for current subscribers to Love Inspired Larger-Print books. All orders subject to credit approval. Credit or debit balances in a customer's account(s) may be offset by any other outstanding balance owed by or to the customer. Please allow 4 to 6 weeks for delivery. Offer available while quantities last.

Your Privacy—The Harlequin® Reader Service is committed to protecting your privacy. Our Privacy Policy is available online at www.ReaderService.com or upon request from the Harlequin Reader Service.

We make a portion of our mailing list available to reputable third parties that offer products we believe may interest you. If you prefer that we not exchange your name with third parties, or if you wish to clarify or modify your communication preferences, please visit us at www.ReaderService.com/consumerchoice or write to us at Harlequin Reader Service Preference Service, P.O. Box 9062, Buffalo, NY 14269. Include your complete name and address.

LILPDIR13R

LARGER-PRINT BOOKS!

GET 2 FREE
LARGER-PRINT NOVELS
PLUS 2 FREE
MYSTERY GIFTS

Love Inspired®

SUSPENSE
RIVETING INSPIRATIONAL ROMANCE

Larger-print novels are now available...

YES! Please send me 2 FREE LARGER-PRINT Love Inspired® Suspense novels and my 2 FREE mystery gifts (gifts are worth about $10). After receiving them, if I don't wish to receive any more books, I can return the shipping statement marked "cancel." If I don't cancel, I will receive 4 brand-new novels every month and be billed just $5.24 per book in the U.S. or $5.74 per book in Canada. That's a savings of at least 23% off the cover price. It's quite a bargain! Shipping and handling is just 50¢ per book in the U.S. and 75¢ per book in Canada.* I understand that accepting the 2 free books and gifts places me under no obligation to buy anything. I can always return a shipment and cancel at any time. Even if I never buy another book, the two free books and gifts are mine to keep forever.

110/310 IDN F5CC

Name _____ (PLEASE PRINT) _____

Address _____ Apt. # _____

City _____ State/Prov. _____ Zip/Postal Code _____

Signature (if under 18, a parent or guardian must sign)

Mail to the Harlequin® Reader Service:
IN U.S.A.: P.O. Box 1867, Buffalo, NY 14240-1867
IN CANADA: P.O. Box 609, Fort Erie, Ontario L2A 5X3

Are you a current subscriber to Love Inspired Suspense books and want to receive the larger-print edition?
Call 1-800-873-8635 or visit www.ReaderService.com.

* Terms and prices subject to change without notice. Prices do not include applicable taxes. Sales tax applicable in N.Y. Canadian residents will be charged applicable taxes. Offer not valid in Quebec. This offer is limited to one order per household. Not valid for current subscribers to Love Inspired Suspense larger-print books. All orders subject to credit approval. Credit or debit balances in a customer's account(s) may be offset by any other outstanding balance owed by or to the customer. Please allow 4 to 6 weeks for delivery. Offer available while quantities last.

Your Privacy—The Harlequin® Reader Service is committed to protecting your privacy. Our Privacy Policy is available online at www.ReaderService.com or upon request from the Harlequin Reader Service.

We make a portion of our mailing list available to reputable third parties that offer products we believe may interest you. If you prefer that we not exchange your name with third parties, or if you wish to clarify or modify your communication preferences, please visit us at www.ReaderService.com/consumerchoice or write to us at Harlequin Reader Service Preference Service, P.O. Box 9062, Buffalo, NY 14269. Include your complete name and address.

LISLPDIR13R